THE FATHER COTTON CHRONICLES

WRITTEN BY
IAN LUCAS

ILLUSTRATED BY
GARY CARTER

CREATED BY
IAN LUCAS
GRAHAM CARRICK
& GARY CARTER

Published in 2008 by YouWriteOn.com

Copyright © Text Ian Lucas
Illustrations Gary Carter
Concept Ian Lucas
Graham Carrick
& Gary Carter

First Edition

Published by YouWriteOn.com

THE FATHER COTTON CHRONICLES: I
DEMON

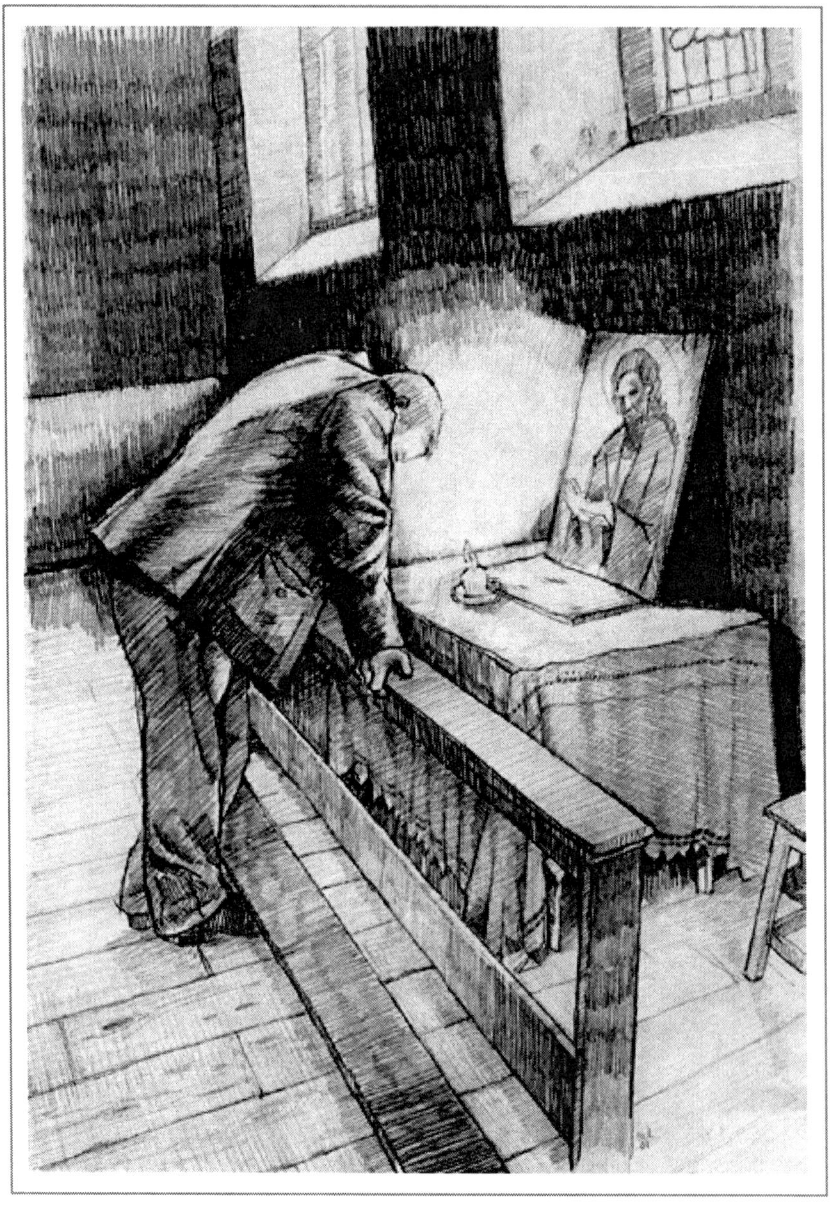

And he said to them: I saw Satan like lightning falling from heaven. Behold, I have given you power to tread upon serpents and scorpions and upon all the power of the enemy: and nothing shall hurt you. But yet rejoice not in this, that spirits are subject unto you: but rejoice in this, that your names are written in heaven.

LUKE 10: 18-20
Douay-Rheims Bible

The Demon sits before me - Unformed: in the process of becoming; The *Man-Shell* near dead, Vacated but for the feigned lingerings of a Child of God; the last furtive remains of dwindling consciousness. He, as unaware of his *Fate,* as I am as painfully aware of my own....

A drink has not passed my lips in nearly three years, not since my first encounter with the Priest. But I have never felt as sober as I do now. My every sense is maximised. I have heard it said that you never feel as alive as you do in the moments before your Death. Well I feel so alive it *Hurts.* The creature's menace coiled, hovering at the end of each breath, in anticipation of an apocalypse. I'm sober in a Drunken World of *Phantoms and Villainy.*

This Smiling and Cordial Gentleman, with a *Demon* dancing behind his eyes, he has recounted to me his Tale, confessing the disorders and tribulations that have brought him forth, leading him to me. He began by explaining that he didn't believe in *the Devil.* Nor did he believe in heaven or Hell, God or the baby Jesus. He told me he was a Practical Man, believing only in the skin off his own back, what he could achieve through his drive and ambition.

...Another sucker in the endless game of *Money and Flesh.*

For three weeks now he had not slept; or slept as normal people sleep. He had been Plagued by dreams. Dreams that had left him *frightened of the Dark.* Afraid to close his eyes...

Night after Night after Night, a man appeared before him, Dressed in Black. The man would stand motionless, and it would grieve to look upon him. He knew him to be the *Devil.* The Man did not speak or advance. But he knew him to be the *Devil.* In this dream, which he described as being as real as his waking hours - he would Fall to his knees, collapsing to the ground; the eyes of the Dark figure *Searing his Flesh.* The City streets and the night around him shadowy and Vacuous; the very *Dread* crippling: his arms and legs would *flail* about him boneless; he would vomit and bleed sweat. He became a beast - A *Worm.* He was *Shamed...*

He now lived in *terror* of a man he knew not to exist; his Rational Self and his subconscious doubts and fears in conflict. Right and Wrong, he asked me if one could exist without the other, when a kind of Evil had surrounded him in the City all his life, But 'Good' remained absent, *Lost Buriedand Forgotten...*

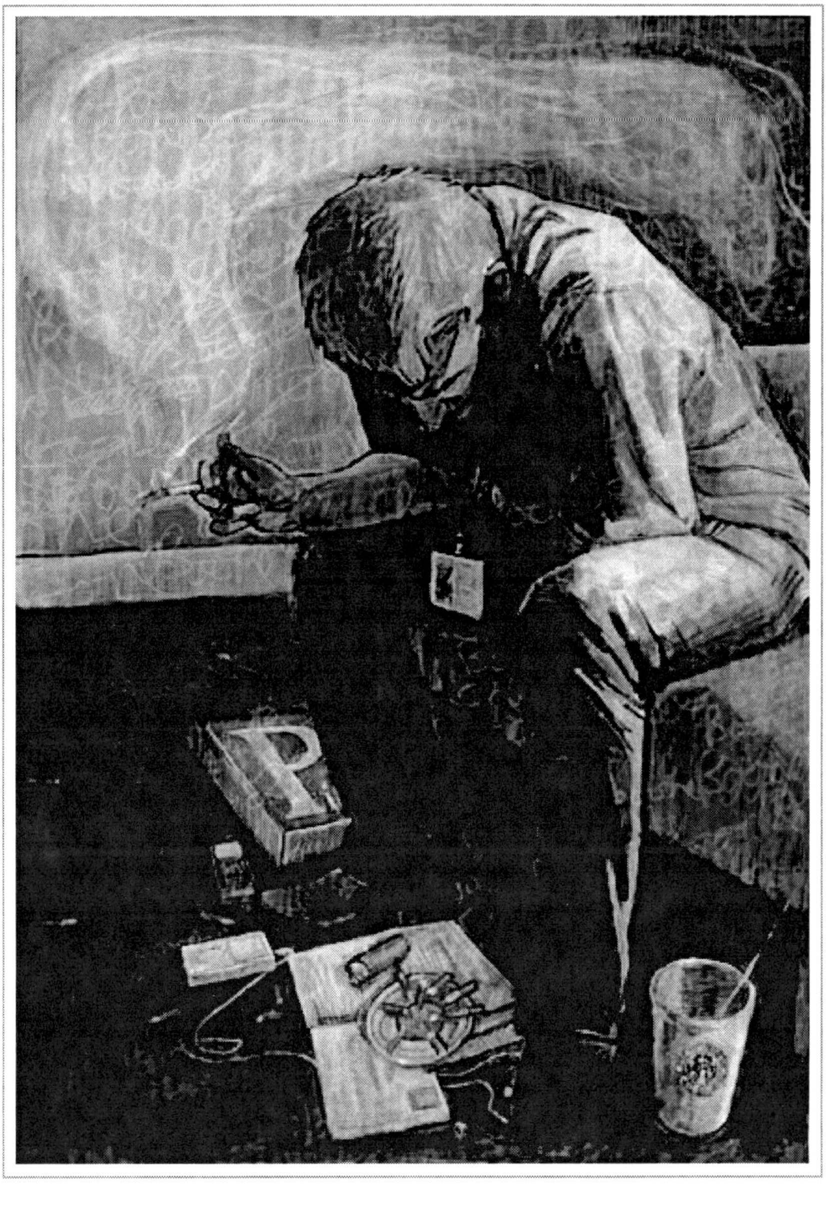

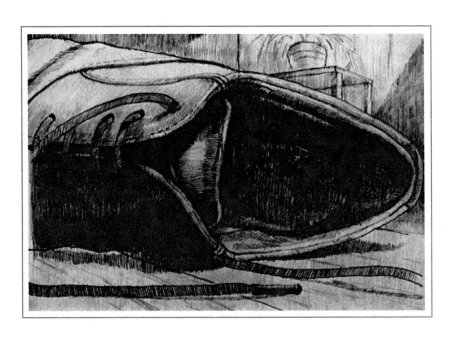

He *began* to stay home, avoiding work,keeping clear of the haunted streets. His sleep deprived *Mind and Body* set in a perpetual state of comatose rigour. His energy *spent* on the daily battle to stay awake. Ultimately to Fail time and time again; never long enough to satisfy his need, only brief enough to *revive his Nightscare...*

One day he found a name inside of his *Shoe,* as if written deep within the Rabbit Hole. The name *Julian Boone* embroidered in golden thread... My Name...

The following day he found my *address* written on the back of his hand. On the third day when he awoke to find my name written and scratched into every surface of his room, not only on the ceiling and walls but continuing behind his pictures, wardrobe and under his bed, did he resolve to seek me out. That I might have the answer - *a cure from his affliction.*

He began Following - stalking like a *lovesick shadow,* until he felt the compulsion to make his presence felt. He lingered conspicuously outside of the church, waiting for me to finish my chores. He approached the moment I departed. I fell to the ground like a Scolded Beast. I had no Mouth to Speak. The *instrument of Death* stood before me, the *Mark of the Devil* written clearly upon his face for any of the *wise* or the *cursed* to see...

Blood pumped in my ears, drowning all other sound. I was sure my time had come. But the *Demon* had yet to *shed the Man,* and had revealed its hand in haste. My Day of Judgement stayed, but lay over me like a *heavyblade...*

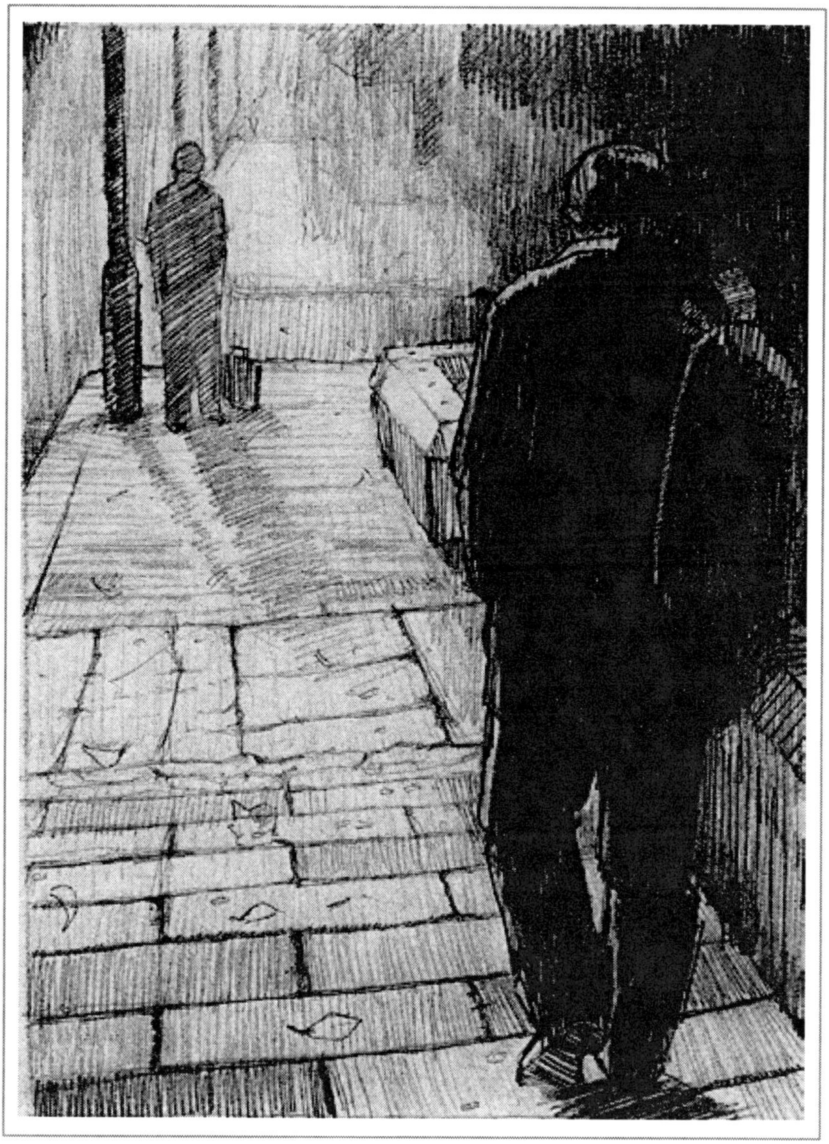

A woman must have been screaming out on the street, calling for medical attention, thinking I was in the throws of some fit. *Sean* came running out of the church, sizing up the danger with quick wits. He stood over my body, putting himself in harms way, facing the *creature.* If the Demon had Broken Loose, he would have been little help - without Father Cotton. The two of us alone would have been *shorn to ribbons...*

But out under the open sky, and in face of the gathering crowd, drawn to the spectacle. The confused and fearful *Man-part* withdrew back to the *shadow...*

Although I had been spared, I knew that when the *Dark Hours* began to creep, the *Death Bandit* would return, reeking carnage. I feared for the safety of my Sister and her girls, for we shared the home of our childhood, that our parents had long departed. I knew that when he came looking for me he would leave none alive. So I sent her away, and I waited...

It would *be futile to run. I waited for him knowing that the Pangs of the Beast* would draw him to me, no matter which way I stood or fled.

...Tonight he returned. Looming beneath the Street Lamp; my neighbours safely wrapped in their ignorant-as-bliss slumber. An *ominous figure* peeping out from the *veil of dusk* - eyes sparkling diamonds from the void. I could not tell whether the creature had victory or if a shred of the man remained...

Opening the door I invited the *Devil* into my home. He came and stood there upon the threshold, and as I looked into his *grave face,* he appeared afraid and lost - *desperately out of his mind.* The change had not yet come; he remained a man, *wracked with doubt.* His humanity visibly ebbing away...

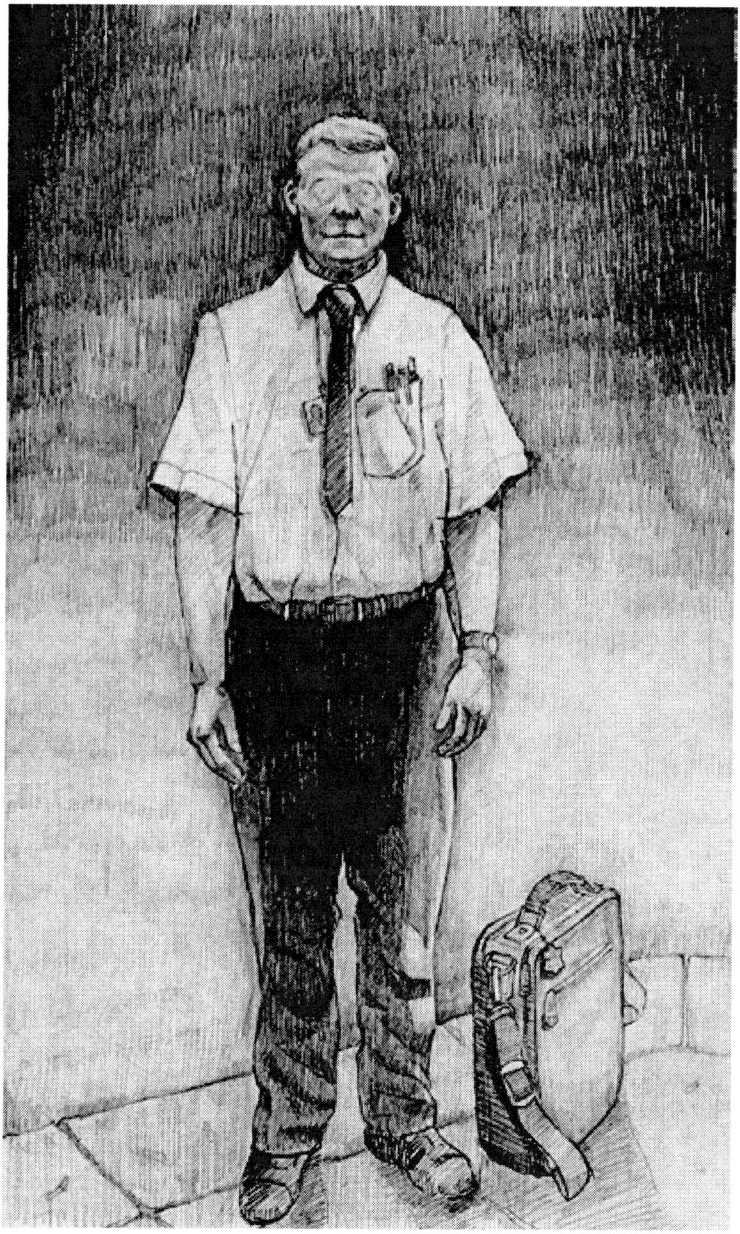

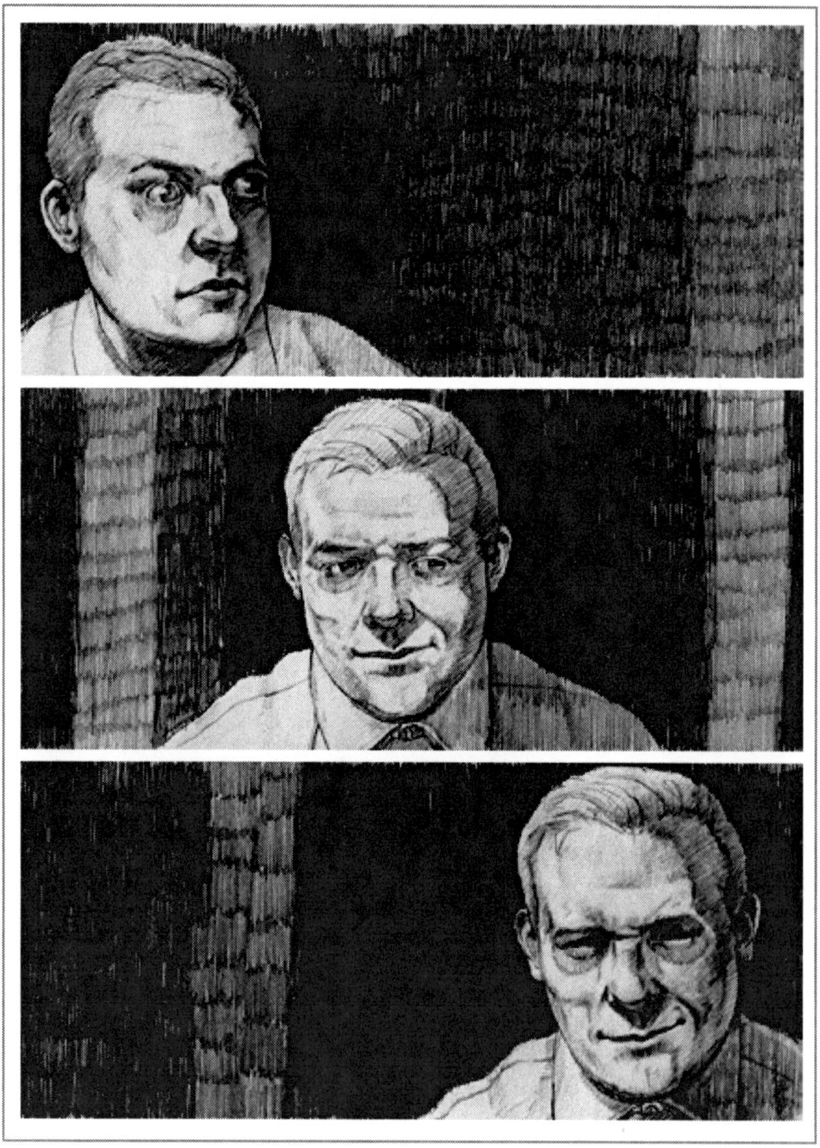

Once inside his demeanour altered, a *dangerous calm* prevailing, the beast inside barely containing its *joy.* He sat and began to smile wicked self-gratified smiles - to the Punchline of his private *Joke...*

He told me his story and I gave answers to his questions, best I could. I told him he had been sent to Kill me. Explaining that no one can see what I have seen and escape *unpunished...*

I told him he was *Dead.* Or dead as normal people weigh it. That a *parasitic* Talon of the underworld had crawled inside and slowly devoured his conscience. Regretfully, I told him, that if Father Cotton had gotten to him sooner he could have cast the demon out, leaving only *bad memory* and *bitter taste.* But it was too late. The *Claws* were in too *Deep.* If the Creature could be challenged it would *spill him inside out* rather than surrender its shell. And even if it were possible to exorcise the *vulgar* without invoking violence - he would shrivel like *dried fruit,* his core rotten. I had seen it happen...

The man remained an *unbeliever,* but his lack of faith was shaken, his sanity riddled with holes. He was *helpless,* fragile, wavering like a newborn Fawn's step son the killing field. He began to comprehend that whatever beset him, be it an unnatural curse, or the braking of his mind - he was *Doomed,* One way or another...

It is a *horror* to see the *ravaged face of the condemned man,* hanging loosely as a *mask* on the face of a *laughing Demon...*

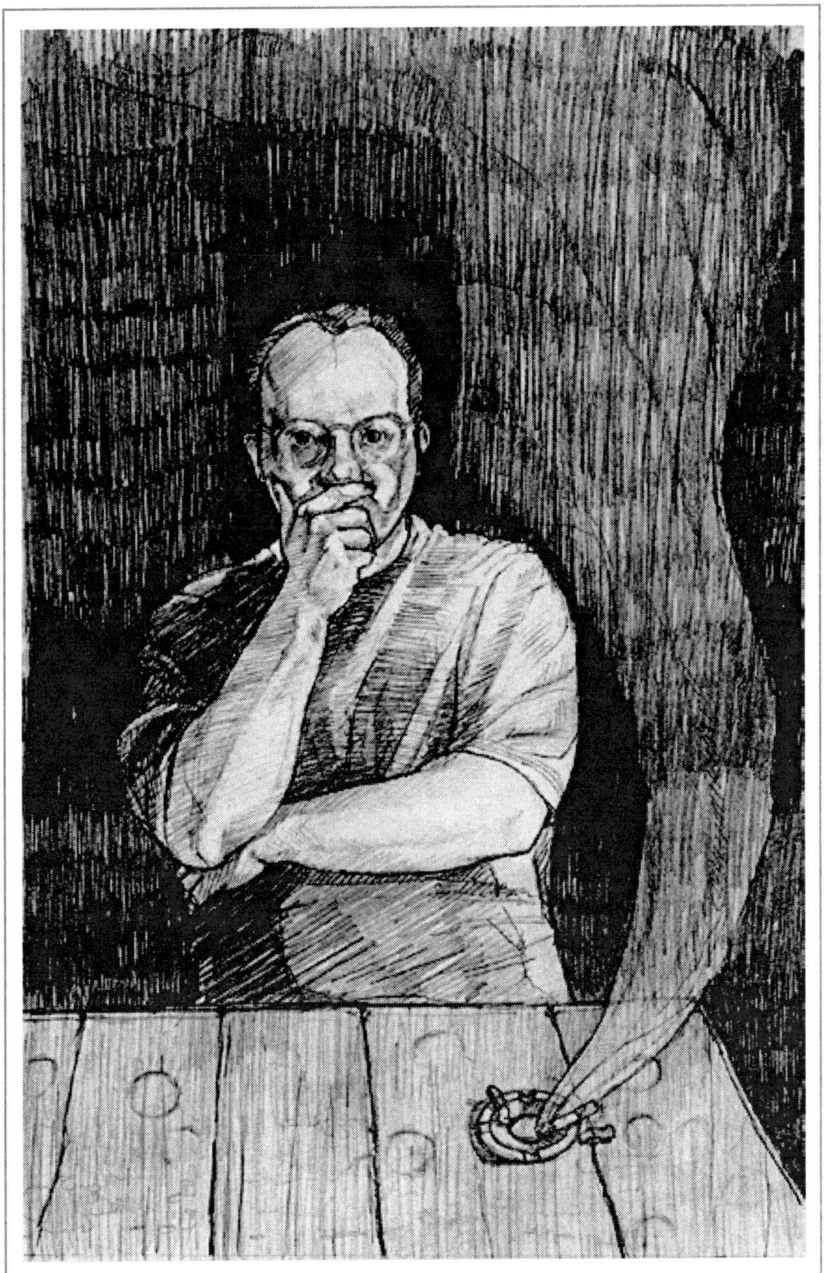

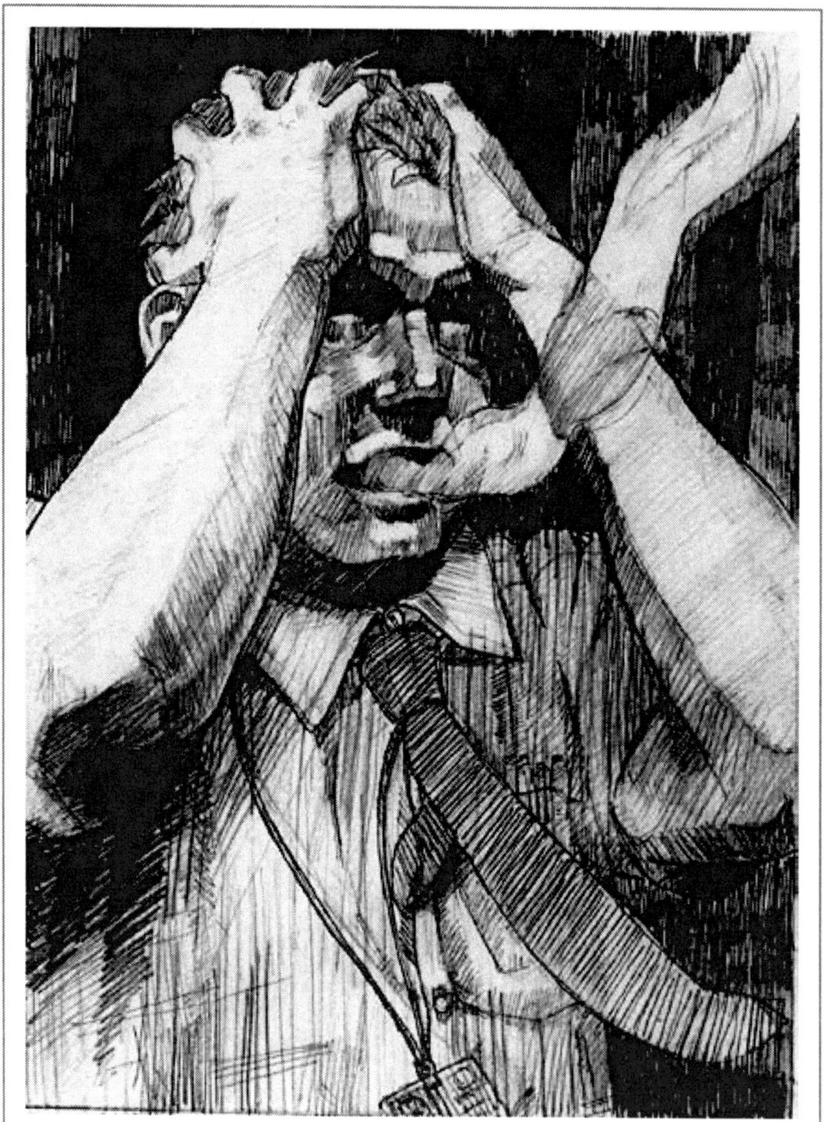

...The veins are now throbbing on his neck and temple - ticking like a *Time Bomb.* Sweat *glistens* on his brow. He taps his fingers nervously on the table...

I Judge it the appropriate hour to introduce him to Fr Cotton. I will tell the story of the Priest, for within are the *deeds* of my confession. Perhaps the tale will grant him understanding - If no comfort.

...Father Vincent John Cotton.

...I am a Thief. I stole to satisfy a lifestyle of sloth and gratification; Maximum recompense for the bare minimum of drudgery. Why work when you can take from those who *toil.* Why Eat when you can *Drink.* Why talk to a woman when you can *Buy* one. Buy *anything...*

I had heard the stories of our eccentric priest. 'Crazy' Fr Cotton: half hermit creeping the streets at night, And the other half ranting and raving, prophesising *Blood and Thunder.* His church was the worst in the borough; his small but loyal congregation always at a loss about his poor attendance and sporadic services. I saw it all as a Charade, and therefore fair Game. It would be easy picking: gold, silver, petty cash. It had been on my list for too long a time.

The church stood like a desolated *mausoleum* for the forsaken; his humble quarters annexed to the rear. Not a soul gracing its steps in or out all day. I was sure he was off on one of his *wanderings.* I forced open the door with a nudge, the rotten wood fluttering into a descent of *featherlike* splinters. Too easy, I should have known it then...

I had grown accustomed to the eerie and delicate atmosphere of *empty houses.* The noises *silent* homes compose - the *rustle* of the wind tapping at the window, the *creaking of steps,* the hum and drone of appliances. I grew unafraid of the *watchful photographic stares* presiding in judgement from their frames, and following me wherever I poked and delved.

In these clandestine jungles, I was privy to a *heightened sense* of people and their little lives - I could take it all in, in one sweeping glance - *the sum total of someone's life,* the accumulation of all their efforts: economic, romantic and spiritual. But his quarters were *bare and cold.* I felt like a *nervous boy* again, as if it were only the first time - on edge, in a chill sweat, hairs pricking up, head darting around at the slightest misgiving, alert as a *startled bird on the lawn.*

I had revelled in the *secrecy of others,* nothing thrilled me more than rifling through peoples drawers and under their mattresses, to discover the *sins* they concealed from their wives, husbands and neighbours.

But the thought of searching his room made my skin crawl - *Made me dirty.* I had never wanted to escape more than I did then, but my *greed demanded a price for my pain, a just reward for my efforts. An ornate crucifix* lay on top of the drawers. A Meagre wage but I gorged on my hatred, and revenged against him for his reproach, taking the trinket and stuffing it in my pocket.

...A sharp violent sound, like the snapping of a heavy plank of wood, *tore through the silence* from the room ahead. I stood startled - *frozen in the headlights,* unable to bolt. I heard a deep *guttural growl;* I felt *nauseas* - the wail detestable. I was torn between running away, or rushing forward and thrusting all of my weight and strength against the door, holding it at bay. I was *terrified* of what was on the other side.

I felt *absurd* - the Priest held no fear over me. There *was* something else. I heard a sly creek come from immediately outside. I lunged forward silently on the tips of my toes, *curling into a ball* and bracing the door - waiting for resistance to come.

After a few uneventful moments, I ventured to look - my eye drawn to the eyehole; the face of a *Beautiful Child* passed by my narrow view. I experienced a mixture of relief and surprise, but deep down within the *terror* remained. Something *unnatural* was occurring beyond the barrier. I heard the low animal rumble - vibrating up though my feet as if a train passing underground - and the audible crack of wood. With all my courage, I pulled the door ajar, and veered inside...

Two children stood in the study, a *boy and girl,* beautiful to behold, Flaxen twins. There eyes were focussed intensely upon the Priest, who was pressed against the far wall, pinned by an invisible force, held aloft from the floor. Streetlamps out in the yard cast dusty shafts of light through the high poky windows, and colours of stained glass played across the beleaguered *Holy Man.*

The Priest, near exhaustion, fought on but was overwhelmed. He was *dragged violently* up against the ceiling, and then across into one wall and back into the other - all the while remaining pinned back against the far wall. Pictures fell from their hooks, shelves toppled spilling books. The desk and chairs lay broken, twisted, bucked and bent out of shape - as no wood can be bent.

Shadows sprang across the walls from the static shapes of the children - Black silhouettes *monstrous and hideous,* gargoyles in the form of doglike and dragonous crossbreeds. They leaped out stretching towards Fr Cotton, still connected by a thin umbilical ribbon of shadow, and were quickly drawn back as if elastic. They sprung repeatedly from the brood and struck at the Priest, his body going limp as their blows spun him sprawling upside-down.

I had been staring at the spectacle in stone struck Horror and Disbelief. The *Plight* of the Holy Man forced me into action; I grabbed at the *boy* restraining him - taking him by surprise. The *shadow monster* withdrew into him; he became as strong as the *keenest warrior.* His icy pincer grip biting, I felt the chill down deep in the *core of my bones,* pain unrecognisable. But I held on, binding myself to him, as he *shook and Bucked* like a stallion.

The *Girl* turned on me. *Her Beast* leap upon my back trying to wrench me from her brethren - the animal unwilling to tear and violate in fear of hurting the *fragile shell of the Male-host.* Sandwiched between the Boy and the *Beast of his Sister,* eventually I was torn away. Reeling on the floor I looked up and saw the two *golden children,* advancing slowly, their Shadow Demons manifesting before them, *Vicious Red and Cruel.*

...Behind them, against the opposite wall, I saw the *corpse* of the Priest rise, *peeling* itself off the bloody ground, as if lifted to his feet by a meat hook, his limbs *loose and retarded.* The *cadaver* staggered, crippled, jerking forward, One foot somehow landing in front of the other in a *macabre dance.* I followed his *trajectory* and saw lying discarded in the middle of the room, the *Crucifix.* It must have fallen from my pocket in Battle.

He moved like a man trying out his limbs for the first time, uncoordinated and sluggish; it was *Agony,* a Torture to watch. His purple swelling face struggling to see - He fell to his knees, his hands reaching out searching the floor, the archaic weapon at the tips of his fingers. Then they nailed me. The lights went out as the Beasts *clubbed and trampled* my Body; the rain hailed down rocks.

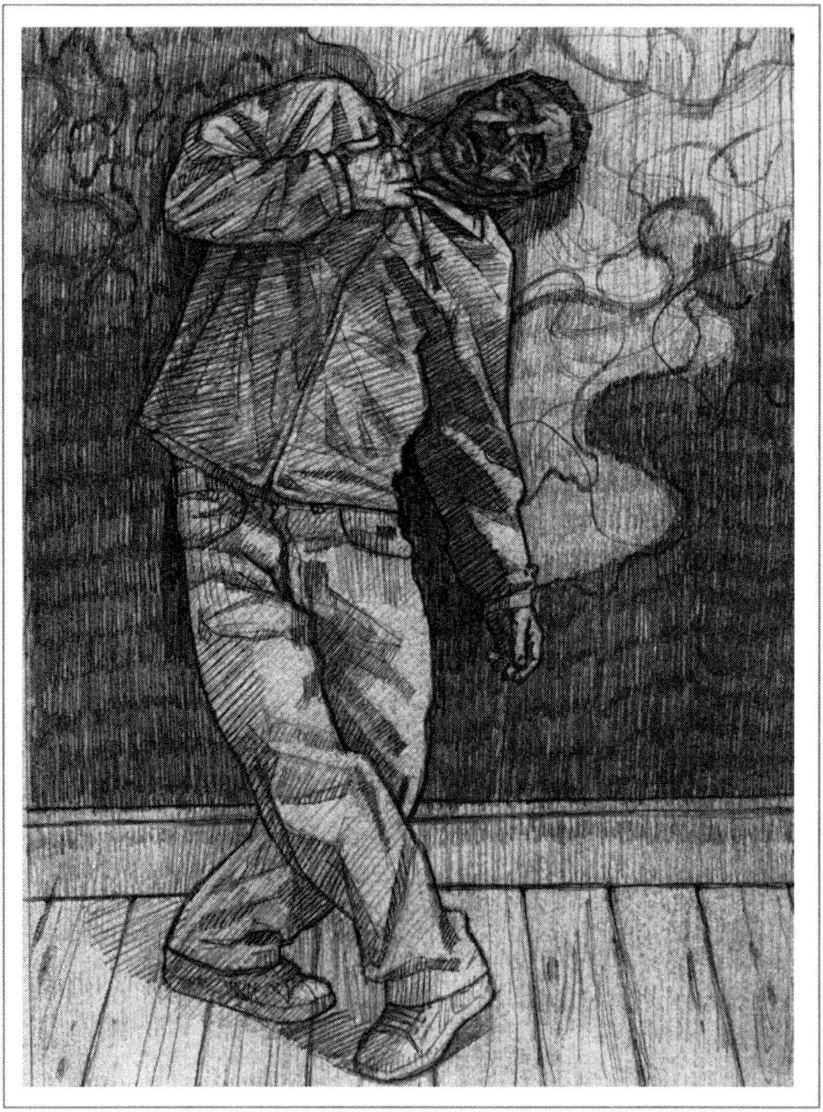

And then I heard *The Voice.* The *Power of Thunder* lay in his Voice. In my mind I saw him lift the symbol and Deliver...

'In the name of Jesus Christ the Resurrected and God the Holy Father -
YOU HAVE NO DOMINION HERE...!
...Lay ye down, bow; shield your eyes from the Majesty...'

...When Fr Cotton roused me, the outer door lay open, the cold night *skulking* in, the children and their bullying friends long departed. He looked like a *dead man,* yet he lived - his *true power* hidden deep within. I *stung and ached,* but I too lived; my life changed, Irreversibly. All the *knowledge of the angels,* I saw in his eyes as he held me, as we waited for the ambulance to arrive. Minutes or Hours passed. And I saw my *destiny,* revealed for the first time...

...Back in my home, almost three years to the day, I look up at the shape across the table, and I've missed the Last *Drip* of his life. *The Demon* sits Laughing at me, the previous face now nothing more than a translucent *paper shroud...*

I am prepared to die, even Fr Albertine can't save me now. My cause is just. I shall be judged with even *scales.* My time is close... *But not yet...*

It is I who now ridicules at the *Creature,* Fuelling his anger. He stands *fuming,* Kicking his chair *clattering across* the room; Breaking the table barrier between us with a hammer blow from his fists. I am within a *whisker of the grave...*

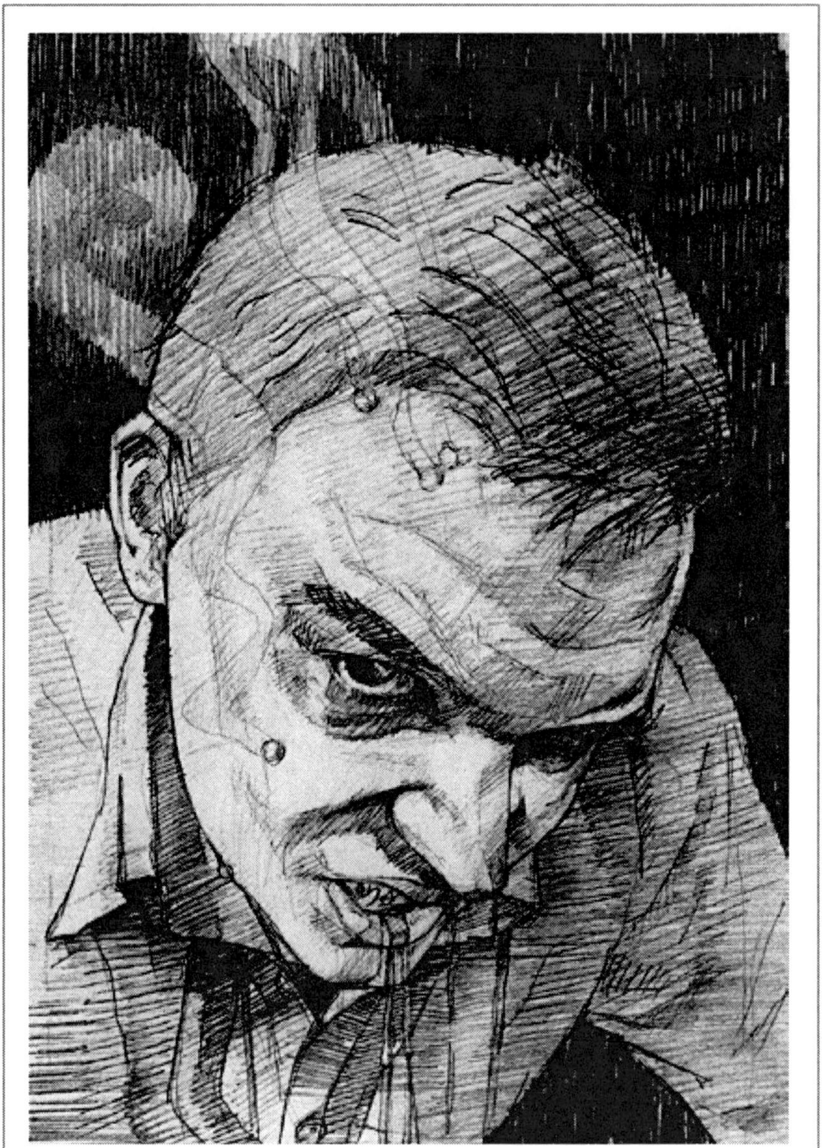

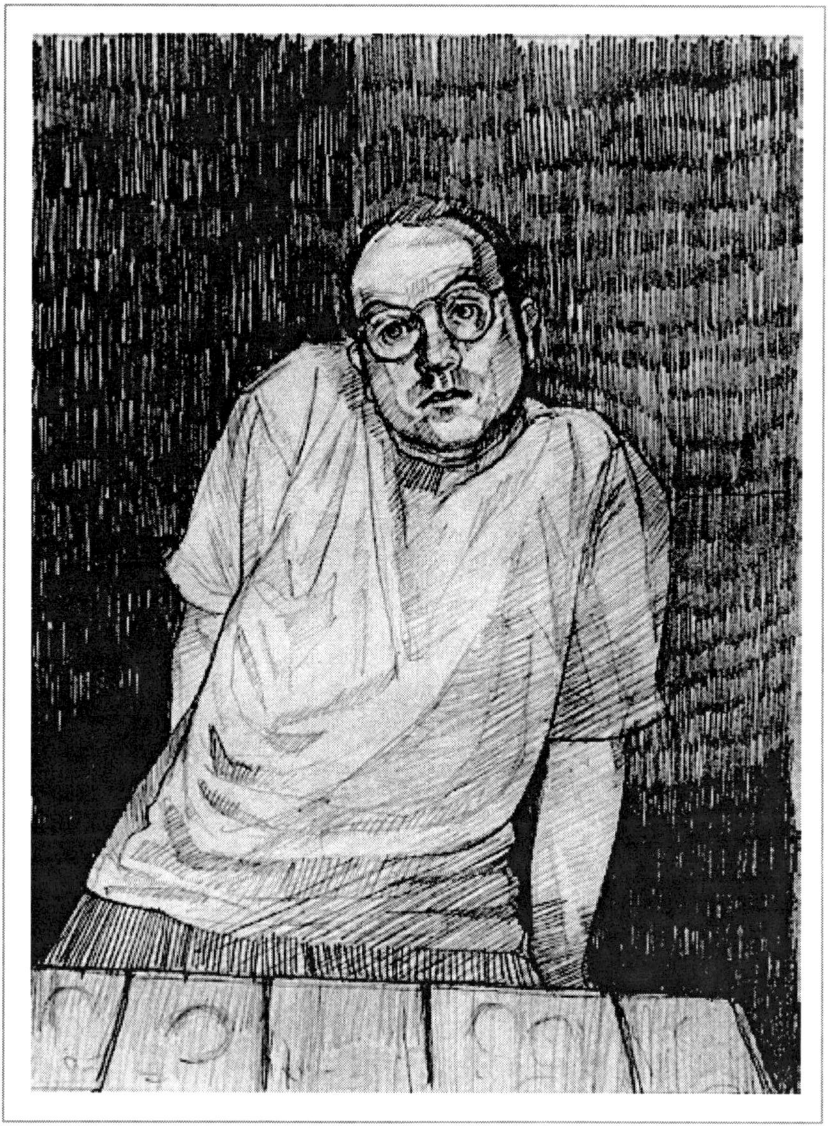

Fr Cotton grabs him from behind, taking the enemy unawares; the uproar had been diversion enough to aid his and Sean's stealthy approach. Utilizing our advantage, *Sean and I* hold him down, lying on his body with all our weight. Fr Cotton takes out his mallet, and his *Holy Brand* - a crucifix welded to the end of a fire poker; a device I had fashioned for him under instruction, to aid in keeping all manner of *evil at bay.* He presses it against the forehead of the creature. *The end glows Red,* and then *White Hot.*

The *Beast Screams* - the high Pitch *whistle* of a boiling pot. The Body shakes uncontrollably jarring Sean and I loose, and begins to rise - levitating from the floor. Fr Cotton stamps his foot to the Man's chest, and with *unbelievable strength* for a small man, he forces the evil back down, and then stands himself up upon the body.

Holding his Mallet *aloft,* he brings it down on the end of the poker. Sparks flash and scatter as the skull *combusts aflame* about the *wound.* He repeatedly hammers the cross - the mallet against the poker ringing out, peeling as a church bell between the *bestial howls.* Sean and I tighten our hold upon the once fragile but now superhuman bulk, and shield our eyes from the cinders and the spark.

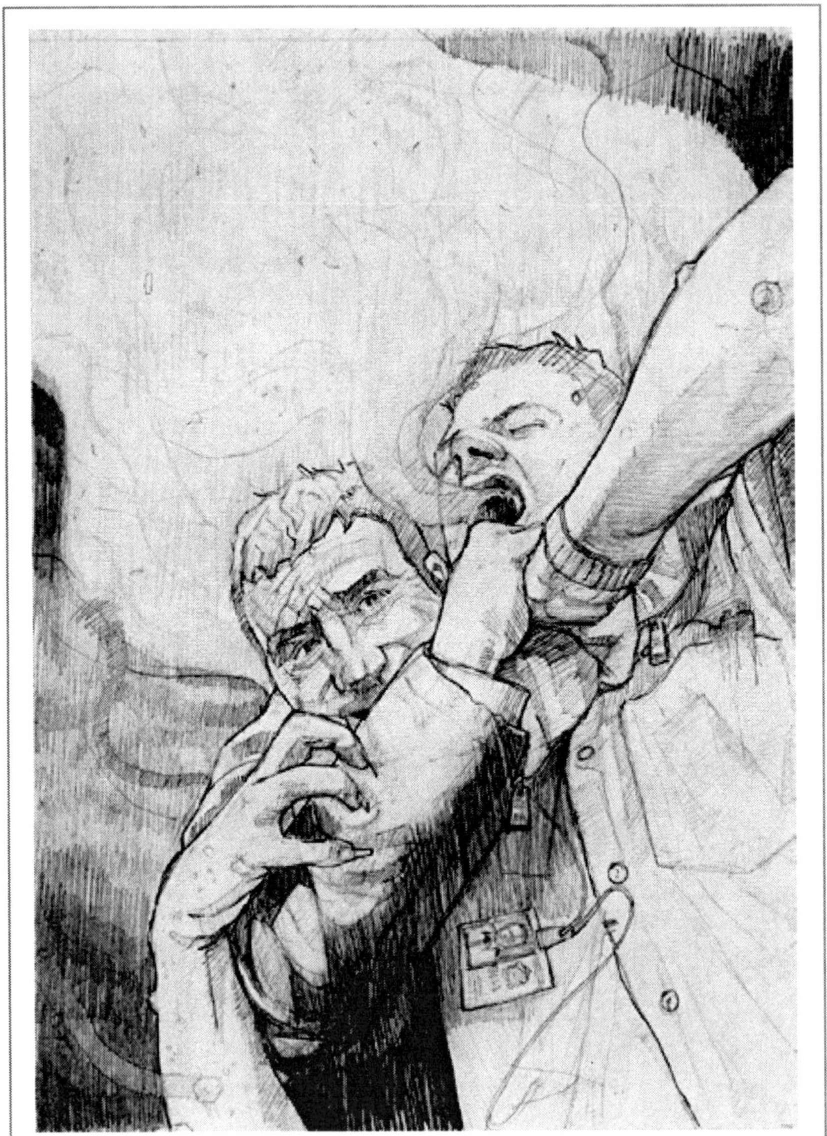

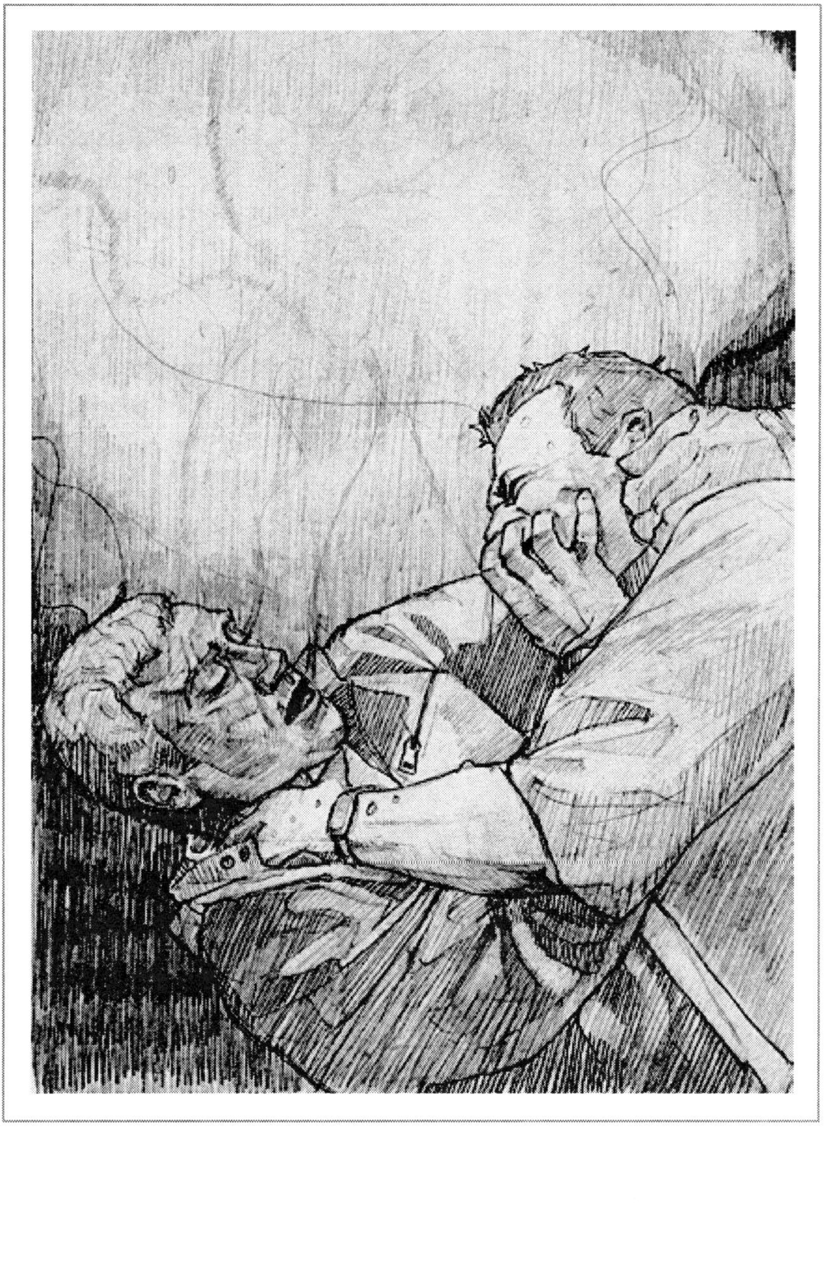

A Witness would swear to *Murder,* without realising our *Victim* is already dead. The *White heat* rises from the *fiery cross* up the Hilt until it reaches the gloved hand of the priest. A lesson bitterly learned: I can still see in my mind the image of his hand scorched and smoking, that first time he wielded the rig; forever marked now by the ugly stain.

'In the Name of Jesus Christ - Be gone from here... You have no Power..!'

He withdraws his staff from the blistering cavity of the skull, raising it above his head - glowing White hot like a beacon, 'Go back to your Master - The King of Lies..!' He plunges his fiery brand into the entities chest; The Body, which had fallen still, judders and lurches, 'Be Gone!' He brings his hammer down upon the hilt of the staff once again, 'Be Gone!' and again, 'Be Gone..!'

Burning embers of ash waft up from the prostrate body and float down as *Golden Snowflakes.* The scene: an *Abattoir of Screaming,* Cathedral Tolling and fiery command. Fr Cotton lifts his might hammer aloft one last time, 'Be Gone..!'

A *Wet* tearing sound rips at the torso. His side splits *guttering blood,* as the evil spirit sheds its host. Fr Cotton *teeters* back from the *fury* - a *rising storm of Blood;* a whirlwind reeling, smearing the walls, hurling furniture in its wake; the lights bulbs implode sending us into near darkness...

Sean and I stand aghast. 'The Door!' Fr Cotton barks intolerantly. I make for the entrance slipping and sliding in the *stream of blood.* I force it open though the winds of a gale resist me.

'Be Gone! Go back to the Fire...!'

He drives at the *Bloody apparition,* wielding his brand above him like a *white sword,* glowing with *glory light.* The *tortured Demon,* a raging torrent, shoots for the doorway, retreating from the illumination, crashing wildly into the frame. The force casts me off my feet sprawling across the floor Punch-Drunk...

...*The Beast* is gone. The door creaks in the *sudden silence* - grinding on buckled hinges. Exhausted, Fr Cotton falls to his knees over the *carcass.* He prays over the *abominated remains* of our victim. Steam rises from the fissures and the sizzling brand marks.

Sean helps me into a chair - my jelly legs unstable. I look like a casualty, scorched from head to toe, *dressed in another man's blood.* My Home, the last memory of my parents, Wrecked - a *Slaughterhouse.* How can Abigail and the children return to this?

...I watch the white heat *crawl* back to the end of Fr Cotton's *holy brand,* and dim - *the light fades...*

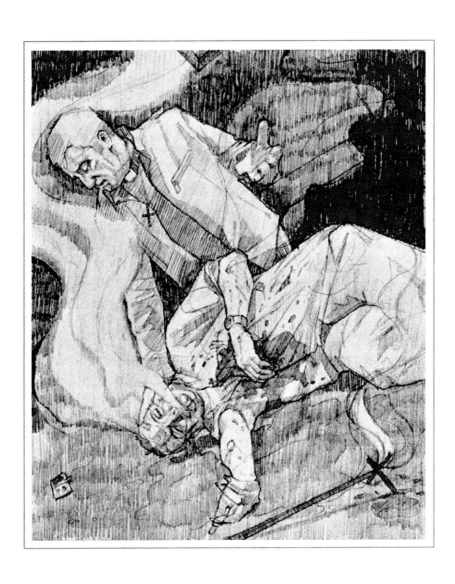

...I have survived. But in the pit of my stomach is the realisation, that things will be different. For nearly three years I have watched Fr Cotton *hunted down* and *terrorised,* singled out and *subjugated. Legions of the Devil's Tribe* riling against him unendingly. I've seen him *ravaged, aged and beaten; Barricaded to Exhaustion.* And now it is my turn. My name has been unenviably added to a *Deadly list.* A man marked for committing *unforgivable crimes* against the *Angel of Darkness.* My fate is sealed. No man can run forever. It is a Question of inevitability. But as Fr Cotton reminds me from time to time - 'No man's place in Heaven is Guaranteed'. And there is another List I must strive to have my name written upon.

*...*Lord grant me the chance to *Redeem* myself - *in whatever time remains...*

And whosoever was not found written in the book of life was cast into the pool of fire.

REVELATION 20: 15

Douay-Rheims Bible

The Father Cotton Chronicles: II
ALBERTINE

They shed innocent blood,
the blood of their sons and daughters,
whom they sacrificed to the idols of Canaan,
and the land was desecrated by their blood.
Psalm 106: 38
New International Version

Fr Cotton's predecessor was *Fr Albertine*. He had been a popular figure in one of the most affluent parishes in the city; a servant of many years drawing towards a final decade of uneventful worship. Then an incident, involving the *suspected possession* of an elderly lady, and the scandal that followed, forced a change in the trajectory of his practice. He was relieved of his coveted position; and yet within the year, propelled by his unique experience, he somehow found himself the chief *exorcist*, trouble-shooter, warden of the gate, and lone soldier - the *last rider* of a crusade, on the front line against the *Dark Powers...* Like all the great *Law Men* he was a reluctant fighter - A *quiet legend* with the soul of a poet. But with this *incorruptible* quality he was unable to turn a blind eye - the very sullying of the rainbow would transform him into a force of *hydraulic and stone.*

He garnered the *fidelity of the church*, if not the reverence he deserved, becoming an outcast, an undesirable; though when compared to Fr Cotton, he was treated like a *saint*. During these short years of service his *aging body* was beaten and broken, torn, punctured and scolded. To look upon him *now* was to see a man as if *mauled by tigers*, after being hauled from the *wreckage of a train* - he stooped bent like a man *one hundred years* down the pit, working mine shafts buried deep beneath the earth; his *lacerated* skin soot dyed and stretched gruesome. This once tall, broad shouldered and handsome gentleman - now a crippled old man, but his eyes still burn with *coiled power and wisdom...*

...The Tale tells of an isolated village, a small community standing on an *ancient site*, which had fallen under the *dominion of a dark coven*. The inhabitants were targeted, beleaguered and terrorised into submission and worship. Over the years the mere name of the hamlet had wrought rumour and gossip in the neighbouring towns. Now the commune became an inaccessible place of *deviance*: no one coming in or out; openly shunned and labelled *evil*. Word spread of *sacrilegious idolatry*. In desperation the Church gathered from afar three men of Renown, and dispatched them to investigate: Fr Houston, Fr Lensk and Fr Albertine.

...The Holy Men approached the Main Gate and Surrounding Wall; the structure had been built and repaired over the centuries by Pagans of old, by Romans and later during civil war; then riven with *hiding-holes* and tunnels in defence of the persecution scored against Catholics. It was in the field outside the cruel gate that they found Fr Neate, the Parish Priest, laced with *barbed wire* to a post, picked over by crows and left to rot. He was down upon his knees; his arms twisted and stretched out in *mock crucifixion...* They could not pass the gate and no answer came to their calls. After long search they found and forced entry to one of the old tunnels, entering under the secrecy of Nightfall...

Under the morning sun they walked openly through the *Ghost Town* streets. Doors were closed to them - villagers hid cowering in their homes. The odd house lay open: entrance ajar, windows broken, signs of disturbance inside - *marks of violence* and struggle scarring the ground, trails of blood leading into the distance as though one had been dragged away by many... All pathways led to the village square. There they found the Unholy Sacrifice: *a painting to hang on the very walls of hell.* The Bodies of men, women and children *disembowelled,* piled and strewn - their blood, dry and fresh, staining the stone steps running down to the drain.

Dogs, cats and birds fed upon the *carcasses* - enough atrocity to spare that all beasts lay their differences aside. At night these scavengers made den in the doorways, sleeping huddled in the cold, keeping guard, unwilling to leave sight of the *banquet* in case their plunder were taken or spoiled... The birds scattered startled, the *clatter* of their wings and strange cries raising the alarm. The dogs snarled and barked; their jaws smeared in *gluttony*. They jockeyed, lunging forward, teeth bared. Fr Lensk struck the lead hound with a stone and charged the others. They yielded whimpering away, fleeing out of the square - but they sauntered around the alleys, watchful and *howling* mournfully to the sky.

A *pair of stocks*, heirlooms of the village's chequered heritage, stood in pride at the entrance to the square. There lay human remains made *obscenity*. The three clergymen mounted the crooked shallow row of steps and entered the *killing zone*. They tiptoed among the cadaverous dead: *stripped naked bodies* gnawed upon. Gallows had once drawn crowds there to witness judgement upon their neighbours, upon those who succumb to weakness; perhaps judgement was now being repaid.

It was here in the heart of the village, the centre to which all the streets flowed, that the Elders and their lynch mob of followers surrounded the Lord's Men. Stones were gathered from the cobble streets and *hailed*. Then commanded and encouraged by the Elders the hounds attacked the shaken clergymen. As if under the same command, the birds descended from their sky upon the battlefield... Fr Houston succumbed to the attention of the beasts, dragged beneath the waves. Fr Albertine broke his own bonds and tore the animals away from the fallen preacher, revealing him *bleeding* beyond repair. Reacting senseless he held his hands over the wound to the man's throat, to stem the flow. The body convulsed; his eyes looked up to the heavens; Fr Albertine looked down and felt the man's life slip through his fingers...

The gang of villagers, brandishing makeshift weapons, assailed the two remaining Holy Men. In the bitter conflict that followed Fr Lensk was felled: *pierced with many wounds*; though they took him at a bitter cost. Fr Albertine was struck and gouged with heavy blows until he turned their own weapons against them; *Hacking and slicing* at each other like knights on a battlefield, the decapitated bodies of their clan slayed beneath their feet... The ferocity of Fr Albertine's blade, matched by his stubborn will to withstand and not to submit, proved to be the victor, if victory it was. He was beaten, scarred and maimed *unrecognisable.* His last few foes, their greater number *massacred,* gave up the fight - in the stern face of their final opponent. Crippled and bleeding, those who could crawled or limped away...

The elders who had watched and commanded from a point of safety, cursed him, casting spell and *foulmouthed blasphemy.* But they had no spell to break Fr Albertine. Standing there in the *holocaust,* the image of one of their victims returning, he laughed at them and they fled *in fear* before him... He found them *praying,* huddled in the church they had transformed into a temple of iniquity - defiling all that was sacred. But their Dark Lord had forsaken them. Fr Albertine did not rest until he dragged them one by one back out onto the street. They did not have the strength to resist. There he *nailed* them to the ground - hammering in blade, spike, shaft and pole until they lay splayed out, twisting and *groaning.* Pierced at the thigh and shoulder, or at the ankle and elbow - able to move only enough to *thrash* - he left them with the crows wheeling overhead, in gradual descent. Spent, he crawled back into the church and lay down to *die...*

The following day the last of the villagers, those who remained well hidden from the troubles, found him and took him by cart to the town. He was healed and mended as best they could, but was left deformed - *so scared and maimed*, and racked with crippling *chills and aches...*

Fr Albertine's relationship with Fr Cotton is complex. He is his stalwart advocate, and only true *friend*. If anyone were to stand against Vincent John Cotton from within the secret corridors of Power coursing through the Church - they stand against August Albertine, and no one dares stand against him. I imagine that many await his passing with bated breath, when they will finally be rid of his influence and Fr Cotton will be without protection - though I sometimes believe he will *outlive us all...* Unlike Fr Albertine, Fr Cotton had been chosen young *(too young)*, Trouble found him. It was natural then that Albertine would be both mentor and father figure, confidant and *judge*. I have always been afraid of the man myself; he looks into you, as if there were no barrier between him and your *Naked Soul. There are no secrets his eyes cannot see.* No wonder the mighty Bishops in their towers of sorcery fear to deny him - perceiving their lies, conspiracies and *indiscretions...*

Fr Cotton visits every week, calling in at the care home he resides. I accompany him, though in the beginning I would not pass the door for six months, after the Old Man first *probed* me and exposed my undoings... We find him at constant vigil, either lost in the pages of *his bible*, or down upon his praying knees *(paining his aching limbs)* - carven still, but always moving in the flickering light of his candles. When Fr Cotton arrives Fr Albertine leads him to his Alter, so as to see him clearer, close to the cluster of candles he tenders, nurturing a living flame for each soul he protects. He places his hands over Fr Cotton's face, opening his eyes wide with his fingers - leaning forward and peering in for any sign of change or *shadow* - examining him for concealment and subterfuge. It is a *bizarre* action to witness, *obscene* and intrusive, full of secrecy and meaning predating my tenure. They stand this way until Fr Albertine is satisfied; and on occasion he will follow by examining the Priest's hands thoroughly - to see if they too have *betrayed him*, as if the Old Priest's eyes have the power to read crimes no one can wash away...

Only after this weekly examination will the two men sit and talk. Fr Cotton will relate his latest concerns and ask for advice. These conversations seem trivial compared to the *trauma and intensity* of the examination, though Fr Albertine's advice is always wise and considered. Their only point of disagreement is Fr Cotton's continuing friendship with the *Gypsy*. Albertine disapproves; deeming her to be *treacherous*; but Fr Cotton is stubborn and will not yield... When I observe these two Men side by side, I fear for Fr Cotton - to see the *damage done* to Fr Albertine during his short foray on the front line, I wonder what bodes for Vincent John Cotton: unlikely to live to be an old man; he'll be lucky to last another year...

These visits are not a courtesy: his presence is *demanded*. Absence will not be *tolerated*. In all my time with the Priest he has only missed one meeting. Injuries are no exemption, I've been known to steer him in by wheelchair, and once even to carry him - the desperate measures taken to keep Albertine's *raging vengeance* at bay. Times Fr Cotton has been too ill to be moved and Fr Albertine has visited him in the hospital, to pray for his recovery. But the one time we didn't show, and sent no word, he came looking for us. And the people who crossed his path as he came a-knocking, told of their fear, describing him as an *uncaged beast*, they *quaked* as he riled against them - *bloody murder* radiating from those eyes of his. There is no doubt that he was coming to *kill us*... If he hadn't of tracked us down someone else would have saved him the crime. We were ourselves captured and in *dire need*. He took his pent up *wrath* out on those who held us, and he gave us a show to *haunt me to the grave*, as he played a game of his own twisted rules with those who were no match for his skill...

During my second year with the Priest, a *Child* was snatched, *Torn* from his Mother as she laid *Battered in the street*. Two Young Men and a Young Woman were witnessed *running from the scene*, adorned as Goths, descriptions matching known trouble makers, the disaffected, mixed in drugs and crime. With a Massive Police Search mobilized, it was a Race against time; but they were looking in the wrong way. Fr Cotton and I knew the *lair* of these deranged cultists, knew that the Child would have to be prepared for *Ceremony & Sacrifice.*

Storming their squat, an abandoned factory servicing an antiquated time, we *waded into their ranks,* ruthlessly, with extreme prejudice, no consideration for the saving of their souls - only one *soul* to save that day. They underestimated our *ferocity* as we bore down on them reckless, no concern for our own safety - we would save the child at all cost. We beat young *men and women* to the ground, trampling them underfoot, stamping them *immobile.* My chest burnt, my heart beating inside my brain.

My fists gouged, fingers broken; a *Mixture of Bloods* smeared up my arms. I was momentarily overcome; one man held my *arms* as his woman struck at me. Fr Cotton dragged the *Biting and scratching* siren off by her *hair* and I took *revenge* upon the man...

A Path cleared. We raced into the *labyrinth* complex, forcing our way into every room, beating aside any who came between. We were men on *fire*: the Priest's actions *unbecoming* a man of the cloth; my own actions - *reprehensible...* Behind every door I heard the distressed *screaming* of an infant; the sound, inside my head, tricking my ears. As we pried them open images of *violence and horror* flashed before my eyes - *of my sisters little girls* - only to dissipate into stale bare walls...

We came upon a *heavy door* that we could not force, no matter how hard we threw ourselves against it. *Exhaustion* and *Despair* began to *thrive.* Under close inspection Fr Cotton determined the frame to be rotten and the plaster wall crumbling. We *kicked* and pulled splintering wood, lifting chunks out of the wall, until the door fell forward slamming hard to the floor...

Steps led down vanishing shear into the darkness of the basement. He led the way and we cautiously entered the unknown blackness, submerging into the *subterranean lair*. For the first time I felt *the fear*. The only sound I could hear was the rasping of my chest as I tried to gather breath. A *shiver* ran over my body - I realised that if we were caught or defeated, that no one would ever find us down there. As tormented *prisoners* or as *corpse remains* - we would disappear from the world...

The Basement complex was a *pit of filth*. The stench of the damp rooms and *rancid* corridors made me *gag*, burning my nostrils and invading my head; bodily *fluids and waste* ran underfoot - the inhabitants regressing to their *Baseness*. Between confining passages the warren opened out to rows of *disbanded machinery*, picked out by grease muted windows here and there - more the bones of dinosaurs in a natural history museum, than anything that ever gave product to the human race... We fumbled our way through the decades of gloom until up ahead we discerned a faint flickering. We hurried carelessly towards the room long-lost at the end of a coal black tunnel like corridor.

...The very candle light dim, as if oppressed by the *weight of shadows*, yet illuminating an *Alter of Sodom*. The floor was covered by *indiscernible black shapes* that seemed to move in the sliver of dark light. The Child lay beneath the bastardized alter on the *soft coat* of a skinned ram, whose head and horns adorned the spectacle. *Incantations* were painted in blood on the infant's forehead, but he seemed unharmed. Over the Sacrifice stood a *Towering Hooded Shape*; a faint murmur, a droning chant, resonated in the heavy air...

Fr Cotton took his cross and held it concealed firmly in the tight of his hand, as if for a *silent prayer*. He entered the danger of the room. I followed, finding a direct path through the dunes and veils of *counterfeit dusk*. The candles flickered hostility, stretching and distorting shadow. As the Priest neared the Infant, the tall menacing figure stepped into his way, clutching a ceremonial dagger, his features shrouded in the impenetrable shade of his hood. They stood gauging each other...

Fr Cotton spoke to the imposing shape in *whisper*, 'Remember to Fear...' And then he *exploded* 'THE POWER OF THE LIGHT!'

He barged the agitator aside and seized a candle from the unholy alter, the hooded figure lunged back at him, the Priest expose his crucifix, holding it behind the candle. The cross caught the light, shinning brightest gold and reflecting the emblem of *true sacrifice* back against the *malevolent* form. The Dark evil shape withdrew, skulking away, pained, momentarily blinded by the symbol... In these days before I forged his firebrand, and before the escalating war necessitated the bearing of arms, Fr Cotton wielded his cross as his only weapon, a small but mighty charm, more powerful than any sharpened blade.

It was only in this moment, when the dark priest appeared to retreat, and I believed that we might plausibly spring the heist, that I discovered the Black shapes around us moving, *rising*, shuffling together in a pack, their *chant* swelling.

'JOON, GRAB THE CHILD!' Fr Cotton roared.

I sprang to the Alter, cradling the infant in my arms. The *sea of black shapes* encircled penning us in. Fingers sprang from the mass fondling and groping. The Unholy figure's *ceremonial dagger* glistened like a streak of lightening warping in the fluid light. The illegible and monotonous chant rose - its power, or vibration, or evil intent, stirred the still air and the candles began to flicker. The Towering Hooded shape laughed *murderously.* Fr Cotton shielded his precious flame. I instinctively reached down stretching my spare hand around a cluster of candles, just in time, as the lights upon the underworld Alter teetered, dancing *abominate* shadows, and went out...

The Holy Man's diminutive beacon glowed orange through his fingers; my own triplet flittered, *precarious and frail.*

A guttural voice emanated from the *towering villain*: 'You have no place here, LITTLE GIRL!' He pointed his deadly curved blade at Fr Cotton: 'I-CAN-SEE-YOU!'

...I thought the fiend *insane.* The chanting stopped, the posse stood silently poised...

'Follow me' the Priest uttered softly, and as he advanced the *wall of angry shapes* took a single step back in their ranks. One careful slow footfall at a time Fr Cotton inched forward, with the Child and I bound in close proximity. The grievous horde before us backed away out of the hateful room, and as we pushed on into the claustrophobic corridor others swarmed in behind, enclosing us in a river of rats, undulating like dark waves on moonlit water. His crucifix glowed *razor-sharp-edged* against the shadow - I watched the tiny candle flame holding our lives in the balance.

The *rats* took a stand, halting their retreat. Hemmed in, we held our ground. The candles flickered nervously; dripping Wax trickled through my fingers, I stifled a yell of agony. The standoff stretched in stalemate... The towering figure hovered *ominously*, flanked by his slaves. He slowly raised his hands to withdraw his hood - my eyes drawn to anticipate the face inside. I searched, but before my gaze could penetrate his *wraithen* mask, the neglected candles in my grasp blew out.

The evil swarm *seized* me trying to prise the child away. I held the boy tightly *caged* in my arms, and curled into a protective ball around him. My body was jabbed with pain, offended by nails, fingers, fists and feet. Darkness pressed closing my eyes. I was dragged across the tainted floor through a doorway into another room. I chanced to look up and saw the Priest surrounded, wielding his candlelight and crucifix, fending off the *horde* of devilsome contours. I lost sight of him through the doorway, the light in the hallway extinguished as his beacon *failed*, and then the door swung shut from the outside...

...I heard a heavy shape roving around the room. I sat up and held the *traumatized* child away from the perceived threat. As my eyes adjusted they caught a pale band of light breaking through a gap in the ceiling, from the room high above: the streak was *weak and ghostly*, but as clear as a single ray tearing through the clouds on a grey light day. Droplets of silver rainwater gathered and let fall from the hole, collecting in a reflected *smear* beneath. I hauled myself and the child into the spotlight and away from the shadows that clung to the corners. Muffled through the door I heard the scuffle continue out in the hall - inside the room I could hear only the heavy footsteps hugging the doom, and the breathing of the child, which was now rapid and startled, his *little heart* beating out of his chest.

The *prowling menace* took a step forward and I managed to discern the shape of The Tall Hooded *Phantom* striding from the *folds of darkness.* The child looked away; Fear infected us both. One further step and I saw his blade. In a sort of exhale motion his impenetrable hood and cloak fell fluently from him, floating to the ground *soft and slow.* In place of the ill-omened robe stood a full-scale *Warrior Demon* - Skinless, twisted out of raw pink-red muscle and protruding white bone; arms long and powerful; his skull more a helmet; armoured skeletal plates cruelly *grafted onto his outer flesh*. I imagined the constant *angry pain* and the *torment* any touch would bring; even the stroke of silk across his tissue would be a torture. I felt compassion and loathing - his master was indeed pitiless to *abominate* such a living thing.

It approached cautiously - circling - closing - wielding its deadly blade which now caught the light as he *thrust* it into the beam, testing for hostile response. Afraid, sick to my stomach, sweat pouring as I shivered cold; my heart a racing drum beat in accompaniment to the child. I couldn't understand why he hadn't attacked, why he was so hesitant, creeping up for the kill instead of rushing in - what was he afraid of..? Outside in the corridor the sound of the ruckus mounted again and a livid banging rolled against the door. Somehow Fr Cotton was still alive and trying to get in - but he couldn't force entry.

Spooked, the *monstrosity* turned to face the door. As the noise of the scuffle grew heated, the knocking ceased, and the *clamour* moved on away down the hall... The disturbance forced the creature into action. He made himself angry, geeing himself up - *wickedness* flashing in the *frenzy* of his eyes. He came swooping towards us, growling, salivating: *drool* trailing from his mouth down to the grime-stained floor. Kneeling in the spotlight I held the infant tight. His blade high in the air, about to plunge a downward blow; my eyes closed, wrapped in a shadow blanket...

A *convulsion* inside me, as if to vomit, my mouth opened spewing sound: bizarre nonsense as though speaking backwards, uttering gulps of *illegible* text. My eyes could not open, held shut, a *prisoner of the blackness*. My Jaw ached, futilely resisting, mouthing awkward shapes Never Spoken. *(I would find out later that the passages were Latin, but I was never privileged to a translation: the words remaining mysterious and secret).* There was Pounding in my ears, I opened my eyes and it died. The *warrior* stood there, halfway between me and the door, furious, terrified and bewildered. He was incensed, pulsating frustrated vengeance, beaten by some *Holy Spell.*

...Fr Albertine. It was then that I knew and understood that he *Prayed for me too... I felt his presence.* Testament to his vigil, to the power in his voiced words. As I lay on my knees in the wake of the warrior, in the *house of evil* - he kneeled and prayed, and *battled for my life and soul.* In that very pit of hell, I felt blessed - I had a *guardian angel*: Father August Albertine.

The warrior stood *impotent*, robbed of his menace -

revealed as a bully, hurting and misguided. Behind him the outline of the door glowed *crimson*, piercing the darkness. A relentless pounding boomed, no longer in my head but assailed against the door. His eyes never left me, desperate to find a way to punish me with his blade - commit *one last disgrace*. But we both knew that he was too afraid... The door broke open, *flames peeling up the frame*; the Priest stood brandishing a makeshift torch wild with fire - shreds of burning fabric fell away, fluttering yellow and orange dappled *butterfly wings* to the floor. On the threshold, edged in flame, Fr Cotton smouldered beaten and bruised, and from the expression on his face I could tell he expected to see the worst: the child and I *defiled and desecrated.*

He drove the warrior back with the *fear of fire*, coercing him into the corner; the dancing light *devoured the shadow darkness* that had clung to the periphery. I understood the creature's distress - he was *naked to the hurt*, his skinless flesh offering no protection. The Priest hesitated, watching the creature *humbled...* and then thrust the raging flames against the horror-man.

Fr Cotton snapped, enraged with me, and himself, 'GET UP!'

I tried to stand and felt weakness, *atrophy.* He thrust me the torch and tore the child away. I was reluctant to let him go, we had endured, shared in a desperate Tale, but the boy went without complaint.

'GET UP OR I'LL LEAVE YOU!' The Priest shouted before he and the infant withdrew.

I stumbled to my feet. Looking back I saw the demon still alive *thrashing helplessly* in the corner - *a ball of flame...*

In the corridor the Holy Man's *wreckage* lay awry in heaps *dead and burning.* As we ran through the darkened building he kept shouting 'BURN IT JOON! BURN IT ALL!'

I dragged the torch along the walls; the place took like

tinder, as if betraying the disloyal residents' who'd abused its trust. The flames twisted and turned cackling giddy as they followed behind our escape... Outside we collapsed and watched the building engulf. Fr Cotton was overcome by tears; *he wept*, and so did I... Only the boy's eyes stayed dry, no tear to fall - but his tears would come...

...In the Days that followed Fr Albertine would not receive me or accept words of gratitude *(though privately he took Fr Cotton to task for his recklessness)*... With the benefit of time I have come to understand the *barriers* he has built and the distance he has kept - he was my angel, in all but wings, but if I was ever to *stray* - it would be by his hand and no other that I would *fall*...

In the desert they gave in to their craving;
In the wasteland they put God to the test.
Psalm 106: 14
New International Version

THE FATHER COTTON CHRONICLES: III

THE LEGEND OF LELAND BURMAN

When he saw Jesus, he cried out, and fell down before him, and with a loud voice said, What have I to do with thee, Jesus, thou Son of God most high? I beseech thee, torment me not. (For he had commanded the unclean spirit to come out of the man. For oftentimes it had caught him: and he was kept bound with chains and in fetters; and he brake the bands, and was driven of the devil into the wilderness.) And Jesus asked him, saying, What is thy name? And he said, Legion: because many devils were entered into him. And they besought him that he would not command them to go out into the deep. And there was there an herd of many swine feeding on the mountain: and they besought him that he would suffer them to enter into them. And he suffered them. Then went the devils out of the man, and entered into the swine: and the herd ran violently down a steep place into the lake, and were choked.

Luke 8: 28-33
King James Version

At the end of each day, whether I'd been sweeping the church, or mopping the charred and bloodied marks of *exorcisms* failed, I'd return Home; home to my sister Abigail and her girls. If I wasn't too late we would eat as a family, and then the girls would tell me tales of school and gossip of their friends: innocent, sweet and trivial - but every word precious to my ears, gradually guiding me back from my troubles to a *life without horror.* The nights I came home too late, dinning alone with a cold plate for company and their clatter painfully absent, my sleep would be restless, haunted by the *trauma* of the day. Those nights, in the waking moments separating my subconscious nightmares, my thoughts would dwell on the memory of Karen Dunn, before the fall - gone but not forgotten, her face crystal to my mind.

That morning I awoke from a dream in which I walked the Post-Apocalyptic streets, and found the last few survivors being devoured by their own *shadow beasts*. Their parasitic manifestations, which would normally direct their hate and spite onto others, but starving now turned on their hosts. Figures wrestled with themselves, like mad people infected with malady. Tearing at their own skin, wrapping their arms around their tormented bodies, straight-jacketed with perverse self hugging... I alone was uninfected and could see these private monsters: ghastly shadows riding on the backs of their *Masters*, turning the tables. I saw one victim running blindly, trying to prise the creature from her eyes, charging headlong into a wall hoping to dislodge her serpentine companion, only to beat herself dumb and bloody. She then dragged herself along the building, leaving a defacing smear until she eventually crashed headfirst in through a department window, cutting her complete, collapsing in a basket of crashing shards... A man dropped under the weight of his Black Dog like burden; *gnawing* with bear like teeth and claws, it began to devour him, and in the process began to devour itself, in an angry tangle - choking on its hind paws. These things I stood and watched, powerless to intervene. A bad omen for what was to follow.

Hounded by the dream, I sat in the kitchen and waited for the dawn. The children descended for school. I watched them breakfast, squabble and play, but it failed to lift my lowsome mood: the *ghost of doom* I was unable to shake. Abigail could read the affliction on me, like the unwelcome alcohol stain I carried and couldn't hide during my criminal years. As a loving sister I couldn't ask for more, but she can give me a knowing look guaranteed to bring me to shame, and since my sobriety she is ever watchful for signs of my *decay*... She departed for work, delivering the children on her way. I walked the route to work, apprehensive of strangers, fearful I hadn't woken from my dreaming.

Fr Cotton had received a tip-off from the Gypsy, handwritten on the face of one of her branded tarot cards: an eye both closed and open - eyelid shut, but dilated pupil penetrating the veil. Her scrawl spelled out two names: Leland Burman, & the WestGate Hotel. As always she'd left a puzzle for him to solve, though it didn't take him long to make headway, courtesy of Clara at the City Library. She was another of the Priest's disciples, but she was no convert or even a member of his flock. She would happily plough the vaults plundering the archives, picturing herself as a Great Detective, and she was. Her skill lay in uncovering lost secrets, the gift to pluck a *Jewel* from the Dark. What she found was a woman raped and murdered, and a man killed in a seemingly motiveless attack; separate crimes but the newspapers reported that both had previously been residents of the *WestGate Hotel* - the only detail they shared in common. The authorities alleged that no guest had overlapped the occupancy of the two victims, and that there were no suspects at that time. The evidence suggested separate assailants, and that the killer or killers remained at large. The Investigation was fresh out of leads, and months of inquiry stalled, the dead-end crimes were all but forgotten... That accounted for the WestGate Hotel, but Leland Burman remained a mystery.

The Hotel resided in the historic quarter of the city, where antiquated edifices and archways outnumbered but still sat rubbing uneasily up against modern complexes. The WestGate itself slept under the *old Railway Bridge*, built into the recesses of the first three arches; each section taller than the last as the bridge stretched out to span the breadth over the river. It stood always in shadow except for an hour of late morning when the sun cut its way through the avenue and splashed the face of the Hotel in rustic gold. An archaic electricized lamp stood out front reaping a glow day and night in meagre compensation. The façade ran the fine line between quaint and dingy, but offered a dozen rooms, in a convenient location, slightly out of the way and yet only streets away from the bustling city.

As we approached the streets loomed empty and all too quiet, the masonry and cobbles gave the impression that we'd walked back one hundred years or more. There was no one at the desk so we rang the bell and waited, feeling unwelcome guests. The man who appeared behind the counter was not what we expected. He introduced himself as The Caretaker. He was a real *character*, a one-of-a-kind, with a snaggle tooth smile, a gargoyle laugh and a caddish twinkle to his eyes; more a salty sea dog telling tall tales in the back of a dim lit tavern than a reliable Host. He looked at us curiously when we request rooms but presented no luggage. When asked about the Murders he said he had nothing else to add, they came and went from his premises unmolested. Our questions bored and irritated him, but his *Respect* for the dog-collar persuaded him to oblige. It was only when Fr Cotton spoke of *Leland Burman* that he began to sparkle and warm to us. He laughed Belly laughs, and looked on us as the misguided and the harmless, 'I'm surprised at you Father: a man like you shouldn't believe in Fairytales...'

He led us to our rooms; the corridors and stairwells were narrow, built only to accommodate working men as they shuttled through; the walls constructed from large blocks and slabs as though contrived from the off cuts and leftovers of the bridge above. These shortcomings were sweetened by paisley carpets and nostalgic photographs that hung, charting the construction of the city at its industrial peak. Our path was straightforward but bold hatch and half-doors sprouted off in all manner of directions at irregular intervals, indicating the warren-like peculiarity of the complex.

Once we had given our rooms the once over, the Caretaker guided us into the bar and lounge; these quarters were pleasant, warm and easy, and adjoined to the dinning room. The bones of the original layout scored the stonework where the rooms had been knocked through and redesignated. A man and a woman were the only occupants. She lazed feline with her feet curled beneath her on the sofa by the window, absorbed in her racy novel, her red heels neatly arranged together on the floor. The man sat away from her upright in an armchair, reading his broadsheet and drinking tea. The Caretaker introduced him as Paul Cromer.

The woman, from the moment I saw her there, I don't mind admitting, I was *caught*. Her big eyes were effortlessly flirtatious, empathetic and inviting; her watery blonde hair falling in no style at all, and scuffed behind her ears. Her lips were so *succulent* that I could almost taste them from the other side of the room. A woman's figure, shapely and generous, not supple or emaciated as was the fashion. Spinning me like I hadn't felt for years, she made my former lovers appear as mere Girls: *flimsy creatures*; because she was all *Woman* and made me feel more a *Man*...

I introduced myself as *Julian*, in any other situation I would have called myself Joon, the childhood nickname I had adopted with fondness, but in face of the woman my chosen name seemed *immature* and incomplete. She offered me her hand to shake, but I just held on, indulging in her soft skin. She said her name was *Martha*... Fr Cotton was formal, she didn't offer him her hand, nor did he offer any generosity of spirit. Perhaps for the first time since I had known him, I began to feel embarrassment in his friendship; I felt that his presence didn't fare well for me with her...

The Caretaker slipped behind the bar and asked us what we were drinking, we both declined, though for different reasons. He told the others why we had come: about the man we had come to see. Centre stage, with our undivided attention, he recited the Legend of Leland Burman, having suppressed his anticipation of this moment from the instant we inquired at the desk, Relishing a story he had no doubt recounted many times...

He described how Leland Burman reappeared out of nowhere, missing years and travels unaccounted for, with a reputation from his youth of *dishonouring* young ladies. He had fallen on harder times but still gave off the superior air of a privileged class he never was, and the *Dandy* he endeavoured to be. For all his fine tongue and his *dash* he was never a gentleman. Rumour had it that his mother was a common Tart, and that his father was a darkskin sailor from exotic ports, or a bigamist night-watchman, or one of many local thugs.

He plied his trade as a petty thief and pimp. His girls whispered that his body sported scars from the lash and scorch marks from poker and brand, experiences that left him cautious. They were terrified of him; he was less prone to casual violence than other pimps, but they thought him somehow *unnatural* - cold, deceitful, and fundamentally *unholy.* His small stable soon disbanded, seeking protection with his rivals, once girls began disappearing only to be found in the river - what *pleasure* he reaped from this none could tell.

A conman and confidence trickster, his great skill lay in the manipulation of others, insinuating his friendship on the unfortunate and the easily misled. Encouraging those weaker and younger than himself to commit crimes for his profit, drawing evil from them and leaving himself untouchable by the Law. ...Finally Lynched in 1889 for a series of escalating crimes. He was suspected of muggings, robbery and violent offences. When they found him they uncovered evidence linking him to the battering of a market girl, a flower seller aged only nineteen, but whose undernourished frame resembled that of a wee lass. And they forced confession of the beating to death of a street kid for a handful of change; he admitted trampling the boy until his bones shattered, leaving him to die in the gutter of *lonely death.*

'He has supposedly haunted these premises ever since,' the Caretaker explained. 'Over the years people have spoken of seeing a vision of themselves - standing right before them; but with crooked twisted neck from the hanging, and a smashed nose, eye half closed all swollen, and a bloody thump on their forehead from the beating - smiling spitefully, like a wicked bugger, an unsavoury look in their one good eye.'

He went on to describe how this malevolence would work its magic. The fiend would begin to speak: at first the words wouldn't be heard, mouth moving silently, tempting you to listen, the strong could out last him, but eventually most would begin to hear his tune. He would reveal to them their worst secrets, the Shameful and Perverted, and the unflinchingly *depraved*. Encouraged he would approach and whisper in their ear, seducing with the promise of the indulging of their every *carnal disgrace*, and then he'd be gone, having slipped inside...

He finished his tale. We absorbed his outlandish claims. Then he made light of it, speaking as if he had duped us, led us a merry Dance; he said it was just *Fairytale*. But Fr Cotton said he knew different, that the presence of this scoundrel was in the hotel amongst them, and that he would drive him out... He glared at the occupants, each in turn, as if attempting to read their minds, or, more likely, the true nature of their hearts.

'I'm gonna drive that Bastard out!' he proclaimed.

The tension in the room was so tangible you could almost have clutched hold and wrung it out of the very air, as if it were indeed *real*.

'I'm gonna bring the will of God down on you vultures' he growled and glared. 'Come morning I'm gonna drag you pigs out into the sun, and discover which of you is the Thing... Do you think I am blind? I can smell the flesh rotting on the bone...'

I had never seen him so abominable, so crude or socially inept; threatening them unprovoked, calling them out, forcing his own hand; I thought he had lost his mind. In spite of his higher order he now appeared uncouth and ill-mannered, I felt that I was perhaps really seeing him for the first time, and wanted to distance myself, eliminate any *consequences* I had in his actions.

He made a swift exit, his words dangling in the air as if from some celebratory banner long after the party. They turned to me for explanation, I had none. He had left me in the *mire*. Yet they showed me kindness undeserving of such a companion. They made me welcome, perhaps overly so to compensate for his vindictive streak. The atmosphere had been roused, Cotton's provocation stirred the blood; but after the excitement subsided our exchanges were amiable, inspiring camaraderie from the spark of controversy.

As the evening drew on, the woman she leant over and whispered in my ear, her breath *kissing* my neck, lips so close: 'Come by my room later. I have information for you... Now laugh!'
I forced out a chuckle and we smiled as if sharing a joke to camouflage our subterfuge from the others... She bid everyone goodnight and passing gripped my arm without the others noticing and spoke quietly and with haste, 'Don't forget what I said.'

...We each departed, turning in for the night. I waited until the corridor shufflings, the openings and closings had allayed. I snuck out of the room, feeling conspicuous in the nowhere-to-hide hallway. I cared not what she had to say about the unsolved crimes and the mystery - I only wanted to see her. At her door I tapped gently, on tenterhooks not to draw attention. Without reply, I called out her name, trying to gauge my pitch so as to not carry to unsympathetic ears. Devoid of success, I was at a loss... Then the door sneaked ajar, her head leaning through the gap, a finger to her lips warning me to hush; I felt *chastised*. She beckoned me in, locking the door behind us; cute as a button, dressed in girlish pyjamas, the painted toenails of her naked feet peeping out. Now safely inside, her serious demean melted and she smiled bashfully, as if she were staying up late without parental consent. Inviting me to sit down on the end of the bed, she skipped past, pulled out a bottle of Cognac from her hidden stash and offered me a drink. I declined, though perhaps hoping to entice me she poured two glasses. She sat down next to me; my eyes wandered around her room in avoidance, she sipped at her drink attentively. But eventually we couldn't help but find each other, we grinned and beamed, looking dreamily at each other without speaking, like first time teenagers. I didn't want to mention her information, but couldn't think of anything else to say.

She told me of a man that lived somewhere in the Hotel - whom the Caretaker kept hidden and safe. She had heard rumour of him, and thought that she had caught glimpse of him once or twice out of the corner of her eye, late at night. And then one day, soon after the murders, she came on him without doubt, on his way down from the upper chambers. He saw her too. She dared not move or speak. She wanted to *shout and scream*, to raise the alarm, not knowing why - except she felt there was somehow something *wrong* with him. He also seemed to hesitate. She felt an urge in him to engage, but also a pressing chore to attend. So in a blink he shot through one of the service hatches to the basement. She didn't think anyone would believe her; she was deadset to leave but by the morning she doubted herself...

As she recounted her tale she spoke quieter and quieter as if she thought the very walls were listening, and in a natural response I leant ever nearer. It was only once she had concluded, and silence reigned, that we realised how intimate our bodies had become. Neither of us withdrew, just waiting; I was close enough to feel her trembling breath upon my face... And then she kissed me, and I kissed her. And all my *hopes and dreams* were satisfied in her wet sumptuous mouth...

Fr Cotton hammered on the door, swearing and cursing out of control, bellowing she was the *One*. I was suddenly yanked back from nirvana. I thought he'd gone quite mad. Martha cowered, pawing at me, begging me to protect her; terrified and whimpering like a distraught child. My mouth tasted of Cognac, a dangerous taste, though I thought nothing of in until I saw my glass empty next to hers. The thin door rattled in the frame, the wood crackled and sighed as it buckled and warped. Fr Cotton kicked and beat his arms against it, converging all of his will. Yet it held, as though an opposing will reinforced the barrier and strove for *Mastery*.

Embracing tight, she pleaded for me to stop him, screaming: 'He wants to Kill me..!'

The Priest's fell voice pierced through the door, '...Don't listen to her Lies. Resist Her! ...She is a *Banshee*!'

I had to protect her. I crept delicately towards the door, 'No! Don't-Let-Him-In! He's Mad, He'll *Kill Us Both*!' She bayed, grabbing, trying to tug me back.

I shrugged her off; she scurried into the corner, curling into a protective shell, hands over her head...

'Vincent' I said, though I never called him Vincent; his commotion petered out, but he gave no answer. 'I'm coming out..!'

I flipped the catch and opened the door. With stiff hand he forced me aside and went straight for the girl. I grabbed him from behind and forced him back into the hallway, where we tussled and argued. Paul and The Caretaker responding to the disturbance, came to my aid, restraining Fr Cotton in his folly. Wrestling, we manhandled him back into his room, where the Caretaker locked him inside...

After the histrionics, and with the priest neatly secured, I caught my breath. I found Martha's room locked. I knocked but she wouldn't reply. After all that had occurred my frustration prevailed, I hammered on the door. Paul and The Caretaker came and stood astride me, blocking in my way.

Paul told me to 'leave her 'till morning,' he spoke respectfully but I could see that he meant business.

'Get yourself some rest. It's for the best' the Caretaker added.

Reluctantly I withdrew; they stationed themselves outside until I was assured in my room.

I spent a restless hour watching the clock; my ear to the wall straining for sounds from Fr Cotton's room, but he was silent. No chance of sleep; I needed to see her. Restraining myself as long as I could bare, I slid into the hallway, on tip-toes not to make a sound; hugging the wall, I crept to her room. Anxious to avoid any unnecessary noise, I automatically tried the handle first to refrain from knocking. Surprised to find it now unlocked, I cagily opened the door...

I There she hung: a grape pecked over and *sullied* on the vine; *shrivelled* - her insides squeezed out; a sagging water balloon burst; the *Unholy* contents spilled out beneath. A Raped peach still slopping as it dangled, squelching chunks dripping down. Her head twisted lopside, appearing bloated in ratio to her now *flaccid* body: a sheet of paper wet and wrung... There is no response to such atrocity; words struck dumb, only tears of *defeat*. Of all the Evils I've known in his service, of all the hurts I've suffered: of torture and enduring torment; this one twisted the knife, this one would linger... To have the promise of Desire within reach, from one you Sorely Desire, and have it ripped from your grasp, it leaves a *wounding* mark.

I banged on all the doors, but no one answered, not Paul, nor the Caretaker, or even a sound from Fr Cotton. I may have screamed, or only thought I was screaming. I stumbled through the corridors to keep ahead of my troubles, insane with bitterness...

Delving deeper into the complex system of tunnels, that wove like one of those pictures of a staircase that turns back on itself like an *endless trap* - Purgatory Fr Cotton might say. I found myself opening out onto a fire escape high above the street, the iron railing no longer leading down but ending in a sheer fall, and instead a spiral ladder led up onto the retired tracks above. The cold air tempering my *wrath*, the vertical climb brought a sweat to my brow... Clambering out onto the Plateau, on the old railway line, I stood exposed, up on high. Although the summit was wide as a road, I felt precarious, balanced on an isolate pinnacle. The only lights came from the sleeping city, yet they appeared distant and below; the historic centre a gloomy and under lit poor relation to the sparkling city blocks. The River a black portentous ribbon, present by its very absence.

The tracks vanished into the night ahead. But I reasoned that if I were to follow them across the water, I'd be leaving the horror well behind... No sooner had I begun than a jarring sound spun me around. A hatch had been flipped up directly between the lane of the tracks, and a shear cut rectangle of light came from within. Out of the aperture a man hauled himself, my eyes unable to penetrate the *outline* of his shadow. An intimidating urgency in his physique as he drove straight at me; Panic raced through my veins, I back-tracked tentative steps, which only encouraged his momentum. I fled; had hardly broken into my stride when he tackled me to the deck. Heavy on my back, forearm pressing against my head; Swinging with my elbows I forced leverage; Grappling, *fraught*, fighting for my life, always at a disadvantage. Unable to subdue me, my assailant locked my feet under his arm and endeavoured to drag me over the edge. I thrashed and wriggled with the *abyss* impending. My right foot loose, I kicked at his legs until he stumbled. Free I scrambled to my feet and ran for the hatch.

Dizzy from the unprovoked attack I fell scuffing my hands and knees. Knowing he'd be on me, I swung my fist blindly as I turned and caught him on the ear. As he teetered off balance, I made for the light of the shaft once again. The ladder was awkward and slowed me down. The Mad Man grabbed at me and squeezed. In the light I saw his face and it was *Paul*, his features atrocious with enmity. He leaned over and tried to poke out my eyes; I let go of the ladder and plunged for several rungs before I managed to grab hold and stay my descent. Unbalanced Paul came tumbling down head first. His body clattered against me but I held on... I found him at the foot of the long shoot, contorted *dead...*

I sunk back inside, fumbling my way through the labyrinth, on, on, on, endlessly scorned; until somehow, by the road less travelled, corkscrewed my way from the top to the bottom, *into the pit...* And there *he* was, waiting for me in readiness - I witlessly hoodwinked by his summons. He appeared as a tall man hunched and bent: crooked somehow, as if trying to contain his elongated frame in the stature of the diminutive Caretaker; he would have been comical if it had not been for his malevolence, and my bitter and burning vengeance; I wanted to *bite* out his eyes that pinned and derided.

My foul mood made caution a stranger, I had walked foolishly into his deception trap. Gluing me with his gaze, he *taunted* me; I swore and cursed him for what he had done, spitting hatred to drown out his venomous words.

'Don't blame me: YOU killed her, you and your Stupid Friend' he cackled. 'But she deserved every inch of it for what she'd done... Don't bark at me with your accusations; she did it all'.

He smiled innocently and gestured with *theatrical* panache, 'I only provided her with the initiative; opened the door for her true self to *thrive* - I committed no crime by my own hand,' he emphasised by shaking his fist, '...She was Rotten to the Core-'

'Shut up! Shut up! Shut up...!' I evaded.

'-Just like you! You're one of a kind... Look in the mirror - She is YOU..!

I toiled against his contention, knowing there was more than a grain of truth in his venom.

'...But it wouldn't have stopped her Eating you in two - just another *boy* she has tempted onto her sheets, and then cut up for the greater pleasure...'

I protested: 'You're a liar! You spread deceit... You murder and pervert...'

'On the contrary: you are the *poison* that flows through my veins... I am only a VESSEL, I commit no evil. I am blameless... innocent - ish... Can you Claim the same Julian Boone..? I think not. So don't think you can judge me. I know your Mind, all too well.'

He pointed a corrupt and accusing finger, 'Sinner..! You're a Wretched Thief, a Liar and a Coward. You've betrayed everyone who's ever *loved* you - you stink of it... You sent your Mother and Father to the Grave in Shame... You've a nerve to even show your face under the sun... And now you *Bandy* so Righteous and Proud, thinking that FOOL gives you Honour, when he's the lowest of the low; his own flock have abandoned his calamity! A man of God in Title alone; without that collar he wouldn't even be fit to sweep the streets... And even if he were a man of High Esteem, you would still remain what you are - a pathetic urchin of the underbelly, a bottom feeder, wallowing in your own iniquity.'

...Almost imperceivably: equally too slow and too quick for the naked eye - with each verbal volley, as each character assassination slapped, he edged closer. Before I knew it he was in my face. I wanted to withdraw, to retreat, yet felt compelled to listen; and it took all of my will not to lean in closer, for he spoke quietly as if whispering *secrets and pearls* of insight... He ventured so close I could not focus upon him. His poetry sweetened - promises of guidance, freedom from *burden*; the erasing of the past, stains upon my memory cleansed. Felt his mouth at my ear, though he passed no exhale to smoke my neck; speaking words so small I heard not, yet was convinced by every one... I felt light as a feather, every breath cool and nourishing; a better man; ... *I sailed in forgotten dreams...*

I floated down the hall weightless, the Ocean Swell sang in my ears. I saw Fr Cotton *rank* and Grotesque, *merciless* and conceited; as if the façade had been torn, revealing a nature *debased and hideous.* I knew what must be done, he must be punished, he was to blame: he lied, led me astray, cheated me, used me. His very actions brought her to harm, had *killed* her - she'd still be alive if it wasn't for his interference; he came between us... The Caretaker was waiting for me outside of Fr Cotton's room, smiling his crooked tooth grin, no ounce of kindness or humanity behind the curl of his lips; he was incapable of the joyful expression without it appearing as ridicule... He pulled out a broad-bladed kitchen knife and expelled a hiss sucked between the teeth of his guilty sneer, as if suppressing a *cackle.* He handed me the blade and I took it without question. He unlocked the door. I was resigned, what was to come was *inevitable*, as irresistible as the tide; the consequences of a life time of events ebbing to one final punctuation... The caretaker withdrew, though I didn't see him go. I faced the door. I remember thinking I was too calm, I knew I should have been quaking, and raging - alarm bells should have rung!

He sat there, turned away from me, stooped over the edge of the bed, almost as if he had his head in his hands - but months of observation told me the Priest was lost in the thumbed pages of his old bible. He looked back over his shoulder in distain; he held me in his glance, *reeking of betrayal.* He blinked his lids and returned to his Holy Book, yet his poise was strangely contrived, as though he were concealing some errand... I stepped inside, readying the blade tight in my grip... I felt a *sickly joy* at the ease of my opportunity: his back presented itself as the perfect target; I had wanted to slit his throat, but this stroke of fortune could not be overlooked. I prepared my strike and leaped for him, one hand out to restrain him while plunging the cold steel low and deep with the other...

At the decisive moment he jockeyed out of the way, my momentum tumbled to the floor. On me like a flash, he kicked at my hand to disarm me. I held on, baring the pain, and then lashed out gashing at his shin. He withdrew... I clawed back to my feet, my arm felt heavy and numbed; my ribs sore from an ill-timed blow. Fr Cotton *grimaced*, a deepening ruddy patch spreading about his trouser leg. Curled in his hand he held his belt; weighty buckle dangling pendulously. A *gnawing*, a hunger-like pang compelled me to attack. As I drove at him he cracked me just below the left eye with the buckle and then whipped at my forearm, going for the kitchen knife. Stung, I withdrew; eye throbbing, *gash* leaking blood.

...We stalked each other cautiously. Every time my courage failed, I saw her Face *wanting* me, and then her defecation at the hands of the *ripper...* my blood boiled and I drove at him again. Keeping me at distance with the greater reach of his weapon, he whipped in an unyielding storm about my head and face - the buckle, like knuckles rapping my skull. Angry and frustrated, puffing for breath, I hated him; if I could have gotten my hands anywhere near him I'd have squeezed and punctured him many times, to make him *pay...*

I jutted the knife out in stabbing motions, but his belt nearly plucked it from my grasp and he drove me back into the wall. I held on to the weapon as though it were my only *foothold* in this world, but he hooked my legs out from under me with his strap; tumbling violently my unprotected head made impact against the floor. As I lay prone he stamped two feet at a time, wild ape-like. All wind expelled from my lungs; my legs were stunned and useless. It was at this point that some small level of *clarity* began to form - my consciousness left my paralysed body and I thought: How can this man whom I love as a Brother, as a Father, how can he *kill* me? Helpless I swam in disbelief. My arm and my fingers finally broke beneath his barrage, and the blade came free.

He lent in close, the untamed red-hot look in his eyes turned to an *icy cold* determination. He picked me up, cradling me as a man carrying his *bride* over the threshold; my bruised and broken limbs burned as he lifted, if I could have screamed I would have bellowed. The pain brought me uncomfortably back into my skin. He lay me down tenderly upon the bed. A tug-of-war battled in my mind: how could I have doubted this beautiful man; and at the same time I urged to hack out his brain... He laid his hand upon my head and prayed for me. From the inner pocket of his coat he drew a flask of *Holy Water.* Dipping a droplet to his index finger, he drew a prickling cross upon my brow - performing sacred words. He held me down firmly but not unkind and poured from the flask into my mouth - I gagged on the purified liquid made *corrosive* and repugnant by my renegade body; and then he drained it directly into my eyes: Flaming molten agony - my deadened limbs jerked reanimated and rebelled, trying to break his shackle hold. But I was fatigued and *feeble.* I felt myself tearing in two - but the part departing took *meat and fibre* by the hand full as it tore loose. The part of me left behind reverberated in an ocean of hurt, yet my body felt insubstantial, as if I were floating above the bed.

The Legendary Fiend, Leland Burman, stood reluctantly *manifest* in the hotel room. Although cornered, he remained belligerent; and he approached intent on entering into the Priest. But Fr Cotton reached out a hand to the Phantom's chest stopping him in his tracks. The scoundrel was thrown into disarray, foundations shaken, realising that the Holy Man could 'touch' him, *Hurt* him. Terrified by this cruel twist of fate, he capered back, putting distance between himself and his Nemesis. Fr Cotton punished him with the power of his words, and the *threat* of the crucifix he held. Without alternative Burman attacked. Fr Cotton planted his feet, bracing sure foothold, and with a sweep of his cross he lifted the charging Burman through the air spinning heels over head, legs and arms floundering, crashing into the dresser. *Wielding the Device* against his enemy (without making contact, like equal sides of two magnets repelling each other) he flung the foul entity around the room: a rag doll in a hurricane... During the brief conflict Burman tried to force the door, failing he made to break the window and escape, but Fr Cotton threw him repeatedly to the ground with lashing strokes from his cross; comparable to a skilled racket player rendering victory over his opponent, until Leland Burman lay disorientated and defeated on the floor. I witnessed the whole terrible debate through half dazed unreliable eyes; once again reaffirming the *Awe* of the Priest.

Fr Cotton pressed his crucifix to the villain's chest, both hands pressing down with all of his might; no fire and searing of flesh, nor any blood: he was no demon of the underworld, but the spirit of an *evil man.* His body vibrated furiously as if plugged into a pneumatic hammer, banging his head and limbs, contorting as if in *seizure.* At first Burman screamed in pain and despair, but his shaking became so fierce that his tensed hard body cracked against the surface and made no further sound. Fr Cotton ground him into the floor; his skin eroded away, his chest caved, and his body shattered and vanished, leaving only a shadow of *residue* beneath the Priest.

Fr Cotton stood heavily, his joints stiff like an old man. On aching steps he aimed for the window. The air thick with *malevolence* so tangible you could almost reach out and grip. With effort, dragging his feet as though they were weighed down, his forward movement resisted as if being held back, swimming through mud more than air... He reached the window, pressed his cross against the pane, focusing his will, and spoke words softly, or words diminished by the leaden atmosphere.

He said, 'The Word of God..!' And the glass broke with a snap cutting his hand.

An unquantifying *essence*, like an excess of gravity, drained out invisibly through the narrow opening. Once released, a fresh breeze entered washing us clean. Fr Cotton stood by the window, breathing deep clear breaths... and for a moment he saw the dead tangled body of The Caretaker sprawled down on the pavement below, before the *ghostly figure* sunk disappearing into the ground and was expelled forever...

Then went the devils out of the man, and entered into the swine: and the herd ran violently down a steep place into the lake, and were choked.
Luke 8: 33
King James Version

THE FATHER COTTON CHRONICLES: IV
BROKEN ANGEL

*And if thy hand scandalize thee, cut it off: it is better for thee to
enter into life, maimed, than having two hands to go into hell, into
unquenchable fire...
...And if thy eye scandalize thee, pluck it out: it is better for thee
with one eye to enter into the kingdom of God than having two
eyes to be cast into the hell of fire: Where their worm dieth not,
and the fire is not extinguished...*
Mark 9: 42, 46-47
Douay-Rheims Bible

We did things down the park like *savages...* If you didn't go
down, if you didn't partake, if you didn't inhale from the canister,
or drink whatever nasty intoxication you could steal or bartered
for, if you didn't pay your dues and bide your time - you never got
to even kiss a girl... And if you didn't show form you didn't get
invited back to Darren's house to smoke, or trip, and if you weren't
there you weren't anybody, and you'd never got to put your fingers
in Clare or Diane, or Susan... Once, in the Graveyard, under the
frowning watchful presence of the Memorial's *fallen Heroes,* I had
Susan while our posse of collaborators clapped and cheered egging
me on, the only moment of tenderness was in sharing a swig from
the bottle once it was over. Our friends gave us courage. The next
time, when it was their turn, it was me in the crowd engineering the
chorus of approval...
...You don't have to be a *demon* to desecrate the earth.

Fr Cotton is a shrewd man: he gives nothing away. I'd
become accustomed to coming and going as I please from the
church, the grounds and his residence. Yet subtly he had weaned
me away from his private quarters, so successfully that when one
day I circled to the rear of the church, hoping to thieve a biscuit
to ease my chores (thief was always a natural inclination of my

fingertips), I couldn't remember how long it had been since I had last past that way. I entered cautiously, easing the latch without sound, in case that dammed pushbike of his had died again and he'd returned early without my knowledge.

I entered his living room only to witness a sight so *peculiar*, an occurrence of such oddity, that my past experiences left me ill-equipped to compensate. A woman, although she hardly resembled a fairer sex, crawled along the floor feeling her way, spindly limbs holding her body an inch off the ground as if some insect; she then stretched up the skirting board, hands out flat caressing the wall. In that instant I beheld her she was suddenly aware of me and froze, poised like a praying-mantis, in that fight or flight way that spooked animals inhabit. She did not look at me - her ear cocked straining for any giveaway sound; her eye lids were closed, but *sunken*, so that the sockets of her skull seemed to be pronounced. I backed out and departed from the disconcerting creature, immediately doubting what I had seen. I quickened my pace, the sun felt *harsh*. I entered the church through the main doors, and the world seemed *strange*.

I saw Fr cotton the following day, before his service. I didn't mention the encounter but he checked me with a knowing look. Later he took me aside and asked me to wait in his study. I entered his quarters expecting her to be there, but I was alone. I waited like a naughty boy having espied some parental misdemeanour, but Fr Cotton confided in me, never questioning my allegiance. He told me that he had been alerted by a local Shelter to a homeless woman who was becoming unmanageable and a danger to herself and others; they contacted him because of the religious content of her tirades: cursings of *blasphemy and apocalypse.*

When he found her, he uncovered a desperate creature, blind and starved, alone in the world. Troubled, she had spent years on the streets, scraping an *unclean* living. She told him that one day she was approached by a man, who took her away, giving her a taste of *luxury*. She claimed he was the most *charming* man she had ever met. But when she woke, back on the street where he had sought her, a curious amount of time unaccounted for - *her eyes were gone*. She claimed he was the Devil himself, and that his transaction with her was unfinished... One day he would return to settle her debt or take from her again in payment...

The night after the Priest told me this tale, I had a dream that the man visited me in my home. I woke to the figure of darkness standing over, finger pointing straight down on me: *a sword of retribution*. And he said *'I'll take your eyes too!'*

I awoke for real with a start, heart pumping, and scared to death for the rest of the day...

How long Fr Cotton had given her sanctuary, provided safe refuge in exile, as a captive of her own devise, before I stumbled across their conspiracy, I was never able to ascertain; nor figure where he had hidden her (not the basement, but perhaps the tower) and from what state she was reborn: how bereft and *pitifully* ailing her frailty in the beginning. How she must have *suffered*, my heart ached with compassion for her plight. Grateful am I that I did not encounter her until near her regeneration, allowing her to *weep* in haven... Fr Cotton nursed her in privacy until she was nourished, until she was willing and strong enough to begin a new life in the *darkness*, until she became accustomed to the *changes in her face*; until she knew her surroundings better than the architect. She had filled her hours crawling to feel every surface imperfection, counting every inch repeatedly round and round the furniture until she had calculated and memorised the complexity of her own equation. No fallen crust could evade her, she knew the direction of wood grain on every chair; she deconstructed his quarters until she could see it better than those who could see. If I were to have moved anything it would have caused a minor *earthquake* to her world, but she commanded the tools to adjust. This process of hers gave her the confidence to know that in his microcosm, she could never be *Lost...*

Eventually she expanded her boundary to the outer fence, but no further. Some of the congregation, from time to time, would let slip that they had seen the ghost of a young woman walking in the grounds late in the evening or into the night. A solitary grey figure, *pale* as the phantom light, camouflaged against the dampened Gravestones, her face a mirror to the moonlight; wandering in a dreamlike trance, keeper of her own council and fancy; straight out of the pages of a Victorian Ghost book. I would have discounted them as a superstitious lot, weak minded and easily fooled - But I knew it to be true.

The Priest's first judgment on me, *his first punishment*, was to make me take responsibility for my wrongdoings and my theft. When I say *made* me, he didn't force or threaten, but impressed upon me the *scales* of heaven, and the consequences of *inaction*. I had to seek Atonement from the very people least likely to give. It was a thankless task, and no doubt one I thoroughly deserved and more. As I walked the haunts of my childhood, knocking on a door here and there, remembering where I committed my crimes, confronting faces I'd seen in photoframes long forgotten - it became increasingly burdensome. I was scorned and berated, some swore and spat in my face, others threw punches I was *obliged* to take without retaliation.

These acts I would have gladly taken at the expense of the emotional hurt: the tears, the anguish and the *guilt* from those who invited me in and begged for their treasured belongings returned. They would weep and tremble, ache and wail gut wrenching displays of *grief*; explain that the things I had stolen were their *life*: memories bound in trinkets and jewellery - heirlooms irreplaceable. Their *intensity* was matched only by their cold steely hatred when I explained that these precious objects were long gone never to be returned. Eyes that had previously pleaded, now grew in *vengeance*, and I was more afraid of their intentions that those who were quick to anger. It was these people who pursued me in a more just and *crueller* way, which led to another brief spell *Inside*, condemned by my own confessions.

There are more demons than sinners rotting in incarceration; catering every malformed conscience and crooked psyche: the unfortunates and the degenerates caged side by side. The *Ghosts* of malcontent pervade the very walls: lined brick on brick, haunting - the essence of decay that's dirt engrained into every corner and crack, the concrete that keeps the impediment standing; the casualties of confinement, released or deceased, they always leave a part of themselves behind, as I did, discarding an *unsavoury* truth, residing there now just another grain of dirt in a *cleft*.

I suffered the tedium right down to the *marrow*, racked with the pang to invade my flesh with needle or blade and scratch out the irritation, staring at those Godforsaken walls, regretting everyday of my pitiful life. The noise was incessant - the rattle and drone, the shouting from landing to landing of raucous banter, and the baneful threats directed towards the lowlifes and the creeps; while inside my head was still: withdrawn into my own private shell. I vowed never to forget the demoralizing stench of sweat, stale, smoke and shit; and the paraphernalia of details: the film of grease lining the walls; the nicotine stained ceiling; the safety net between levels infused with a fine layer of hair like fuzz... and the fucking *cockroaches!* They came at night. I'd watch them scurry in the gap under the door, a late night horror show; wagering myself their size only from the length of their antennae. They were the real occupants of the stone jungle.

Two men shared my tight cell, a wife-murderer, and a Mental asylum *loony toon* called Kevin who'd never shut up, pacing our tiny floorspace counting his steps, only stopping every revolution to ask "Where's John..? Where's John?" I'd tell him only to forget by the time he'd gone round again. The murderer on the other hand was of a different sort, though he was only a college lecturer, we called him *The Professor*; he'd extinguished his adulteress lover in a rage of jealousy. It was a stroke of fortune that he recognised within me a latent potential. He told me stories from the books he read, to encourage me to try one. I found most too hard and was discouraged, until he introduced me to 'The Strange Case of Dr Jekyll and Mr Hyde' by Robert Louis Stevenson. I may not have understood every word, but it was as though it had been written for me to find.

When the bottled pressure threatened the *bends*, and I was given to *curse* the *Priest*, it served me well to remember he was affecting me to save my soul. When I was released I left the burden behind, I paid a debt I owed myself, and appeased those I had wronged. However there are consequences in this life for trying to *cleanse* your soul for the next. I was shunned, tainted, stigmatized and unemployable. It was only the persuasive powers of the Priest, his promises and assurance, which persuaded my sister to finally allow my return. The neighbours scorned me as an undesirable, my parent's old friends muttered of the disappointment I was them, *'They'll be turning in their graves!'* and my friends, on both sides of the law, ostracised me for betrayal. I was labelled a Coward, a Traitor, Ignorant, Selfish and *Scum...*

Early in their friendship Fr Albertine presented Fr Cotton with an antique box, from which he removed a wrapped bundle of ornate cloth, unravelling the sumptuous fabric with reverence and ceremony, as if it were the *Robe* of the Christ, to reveal a glistening *bayonet.* His Grandfather had taken if from a German officer in the Great War. It was Gladius wide and long, a weapon for slashing as opposed to piercing, with knife point and a serrated edge running along the underside near the handle. And then from the chest he gingerly lifted a *Black Gun*. This had been his Father's Service Revolver from the 2nd War. Fr Albertine had bent these corruptors to his cause and they had taken down many an enemy by his hand. They were his legacy, and he was not only passing them on to Fr Cotton as if his heir, but he was also passing on the baton - Fr Cotton would now lead the fight.

He placed the gun in the Priest's hand, but held on firmly, locking his friend with a stern hurtful eye. 'They have served me well... For there are times my Son, when the power of the Cross isn't enough to deter the Heathen and the Beast...'

Confessing to his young protégé, the roles reversed, he recounted the tale of the *Riverside Wolf*. This was the name the Newspapers had given the unknown assailant who stalked the streets when Albertine himself was only a young priest. Over a period of two and a half months three bodies were discovered, one surfaced in the river, and two more under the shadow of the bridges. All women and all *defaced*. The Wolf preyed on those alone at night, bludgeoning from behind and dragging out of sight, where he would remove their pretty features, disfiguring them unrecognisable with his bare hands (and destroying their eyes which judged him so). His final flurry would be to lift their skirts and expose their private slits in *disgrace*.

Fr Albertine feared for those under his protection, hysteria in the city was palpable. None felt safety in their comforts. He resolved to catch the monster himself. He trailed the streets and alleys of the waterfront for weeks without sign or sound. No new crimes were committed, unsurprising with everyone afraid to venture out at night. He was cautious, worried he was setting himself up to take the blame, but true to his defining nature - he could not step aside and allow this villain to harvest. The nights grew long and frosty; he fretted about the onset of winter, and if his *game* would hibernate far from his clutches. He struck fortune upon the quayside on a blustery night, where the gusts *masked* all other sounds, and he braced himself back against a wall to escape the accursed draft. From his sheltered position, looking out across the boards and bare bones of the market stalls that had flourished earlier in the day, where people had subsided their fears for the safety of the autumn light - there he saw an entity move amongst the *waste. A man-thing that crawled*, scavenging the scraps and *rot* discarded by the grocers and the butchers. Albertine watched this WaterRat tuck away his bundle and scuttle to the edge, where the river flowed black and choppy, and disappear over the rim.

Braking from cover Fr Albertine scampered best he could against the wind lest the vermin should escape. He found a ladder leading down, one of many spaced along the front for the serving of small boats. Reluctantly he descended, the watery fall uninviting. He glimpsed a narrow ledge connecting the immense beams that held the quay aloft. He leapt the small distance onto the uneven boards which followed on deep into the wooden cavern. The wind whistled though the apertures and the cold tide snapped like icy-fire at his steps. Daring to tread his feet into the imposing darkness, he was relieved to discover shafts of corpse light smoking down through fissures lanced here and there in the knots and wood grain above. The path twisted, hugging the deep rooted foundations, dangerous as a train line where the cross beams are too few and far between. At last he drew close to a *loathsome nest*; woven from the discarded, secreted across a wider platform. And there at its centre sat the *Wolf*, the name wholly inappropriate - this unfortunate was more salamander, slime smeared over amphibious anaemic skin; and young, a teenager with a meagre growth of hair upon his chin.

The howling gust colluded in Albertine's stealthy approach. As he closed, he watched the creature nibble on the undelicacies he'd scavenged, and saw, about the nest, the trophies the Wolf had taken - the faces and the fragments he had peeled away. Albertine wanted to *vomit*, he bent over *retching* but nothing came; it was his first taste of sick morality, and he vowed to slay the degenerate in *cold blood,* planting a bullet between his ears; the forgiveness of his profession, *unforgivably* absent. From under his coat he drew his revolver with purpose and straightened his sickened stomach upright. *The wolf was gone...* Although he had the gun Albertine was afraid, he was in the murderer's *lair* and had to escape. He backed away but couldn't trust his feet without looking for his footfalls. He reholstered his firearm, turned and tried to quicken his pace, knowing the risk of a loose step. Round and round snaking the beams he went, aware of the open river ahead. The unseen figure pulled aside a plank and Albertine's trajectory careened forward, he fell unbalanced only to catch himself, paining a desperate hold on the timber before him as his legs and body plummeted into the *icy black* waters below. The ferocity of the Wolf came on, slashing at his hold with his razor sharp nails, leaving Albertine hanging by one arm grappled to the plank. The waters felt as if they were trying to suck him down, while the unkind temperature numbed his limbs as if a slow rising poison. The *fiend* bared his rotting partial teeth, and went for the Priest's anchoring brace. Albertine pulled his gun from its sheath with his weaker gorged arm and fired up frantically, hitting the Wolf several times from close range but also grazing his own supporting arm in the process. He plunged into the *dark blanket*, with the *monster* following after; he felt limbs brushing against his own and grasping emptily - and then it was gone, compelled down into the deep. Albertine was bounced and swirled against the beams and dragged far away out into the river...

He may have felt like he'd drank the ocean but he didn't drown. He was able to grab the lines of a ported fishing boat down stream, until he regained his strength, and climb his way back onto the dock. He saved the gun from the deep; the weapon was *treacherous,* but he owed it an honest debt. The following day he revisited the nest, but found no sign of the *WaterRat.* The savage-spree brought to an end, the crimes were left unsolved, but the experience greatly troubled the Priest. He spent the following decades within the bonds of regular worship, shying away from action, placing his faith in prayer. His shooting of *The Riverside Wolf* he'd kept secret, until he handed the *guilty* instrument on to his successor.

Much to my surprise and lasting resentment, Fr Albertine approved of Catherine. How he could trust her when so little was known about her *mysterious* and guarded past, only he could say. He fondly nicknamed her Lucy, after the Saint martyred for her faith. *Lucia* was threatened with defilement in a brothel unless she recanted. The old Priest spoke her words:

'No one's body is polluted so as to endanger the soul if it has not pleased the mind. If you were to lift my hand to your idol and so make me offer against my will, I would still be guiltless in the sight of the true God, who judges according to the will and knows all things. If now, against my will, you cause me to be polluted, a twofold purity will be gloriously imputed to me. You cannot bend my will to your purpose; whatever you do to my body, that cannot happen to me.'

So they tortured her and stabbed out her eyes, only for God to endow her the gift of sight without eyes. From his revered books Fr Albertine revealed images of the Saint, depicted each time holding out her *severed eyes on a golden plate*.

When the time was judged right, like a debutant, Catherine was presented into our congregation. She was given the position of live-in housekeeper; she was to clean his quarters and prepare his meals (although she is in truth a terrible cook). I was still to clean the church, maintain the grounds, and fulfil any handyman jobs required. When my *covert* duties led me away, she cleaned the church in my stead, achieving a standard higher than my own - embarrassingly outperformed by a *blind girl*.

Fr Cotton was able to behave in ways a normal priest could

not. If someone had complained, reporting him for sharing rooms with a single woman of *questionable* background, what would his superiors have done? They would turn a *blind eye*, because who else were they to send out into the night, to take on the *servants of evil*, to kill those whom the church itself would dare not *name* in public. But he wanted to protect her from his sideline occupation, so we did not involve her in our schemes, and he tried not to bring his troubles home.

Catherine took in a stray, an unhandsome cat that had *haunted* the grounds as long as I can remember. It was a skinny white thing with black patches splashed across its face and back - as though afflicted with an accursed birthmark. At once akin, she fed and pampered the tom, inviting him in with impunity - a stray taking in a stray. Yet he always remained an untamed creature, and reviled Fr Cotton, and the Priest had no love for it. If he came upon the trespasser in the rectory, it would hiss at him, its coat standing out straight spiky as a lion fish, prepared to pounce, only to turn and scarper in fear of the master of the house.

Catherine was inclined to hum to herself as she set about her menial tasks: toying with elaborate melodies and tapping out unconventional rhythms on her fingers. At first I thought it just to disguise the counting of her footsteps, or to calculate the distance from her folk to the salt. When listening to Fr Cotton's gramophone in the evening, he'd *catch* her gesturing extravagantly to and fro with her arm in hypnotic display. This went on for several weeks before he finally cracked her *code*. Somehow he procured and gifted her a second hand *cello*, which to his surprise she could play *flawlessly* - accompanying his records by ear and haunting adagios from memory. Scratched and mistreated the instrument had an *abusive* history of its own; she would absently caress its hurts with her fingertips, empathising with the pain.

My sister Abigail had a complicated relationship with the Priest. She held a grudge against him for persuading her to take me back in, only to lead me astray, into a harm's way she couldn't understand but whose consequences troubled her as the regularity of my injuries mounted. She saw him as no better than the associates from my unacceptable past, worse in fact because he fell under the umbrella of formal respectability, and she distrusted the *vanity* and *piety* she associated with the Church. Things remained frosty between them, but once he discovered she had piano lessons as a girl, he paid her a visit and asked kindly enough for her to consent to play for his blind companion. The organist at church was a mean spirited, stubborn, *rotund* woman old before her time; she was territorial to a fault and refused point blank to entertain Catherine, having taken an immediate dislike *Vincent's Broken Angel*; she was, like many, jealous of this interloper's intimacy with the Priest.

Abigail dressed her girls in their *Sunday* best for the occasion, and we all gathered in his parlour for the performance. My sister played proficiently though she was rusty and no match for Catherine, but the piano complimented her cello well. While playing Catherine was struck *beautiful*, as if she'd just stepped out of a sumptuous canvas, one painted by a pre-Raphaelite eye; and her music sang in a voice as if channelled straight from on high... The evening harvested an almost sisterly bond between the two women. Abigail's girls were initially apprehensive of Catherine's *affliction*, but soon warmed to her capacity to invoke her childlike side; they related to her as one of them, inhabiting the secret realm, separate from the adult world. Playing hide and seek they'd marvel at how they could never escape her, as if by magic there was no hiding place she couldn't find. For a time Abigail held the misguided assumption that Catherine would be my perfect spouse, bringing an end to my disagreeable ways, but I knew she only had *unseeing* eyes for the Priest.

Fr Cotton provided Catherine with clothes from the church's

charity bag, they were old women's clothes, unflattering and out of style. After taking one look at her, Abigail donated a generous supply from her own closet, items dating from before her children notched her up a dress size... Stumbling upon her in the kitchen, seeing her dressed as my sister for the first time - in bloom, her hair brushed per instruction, styled *sensuously* over her sunken eyes, more akin to a *forties movie star*; a mask of prettiness to seek favour with the Priest. She even wore earrings and a necklace of my mother's, not expensive or precious, those Abigail kept for herself and the girls, but signifiers of my departed parents nevertheless. Feminine clothes flaunted Catherine as a *Woman*, clinging to her slender frame, accentuating her *feline* gifts; and though in them she seemed to flower, they also revealed the history of *scars* upon her arms and shoulders, defacing her pale skin.

These marks were unmistakably *self-inflicted*, rows of healed slices and cigarette burns; inscribing her hurts in a short-hand language only she could read; a kind of tattooed lady, only where the blood-ink is washed away and leaves the imprint, a memory in the wad of paper of where the pencil has been. Some of her blemishes appeared considered, methodical, equally spaced and sized, but others hacked diagonally and haphazard out of control, sneaking under her arms and thighs, continuing unseen beneath her clothes; a product of *Cruel* masochism or misdirected sadism for another she could only turn on herself. Fr Cotton asked me not to speak of them, even though she wore them openly, not in defiance, but unstigmatized - blind to there affect. No new wounds were to be seen, evidence that her emancipation had eased her woes. She even persuaded him to discard the glove that protected his own burn-scarred hand from harsh eyes, encouragement him to wear the *mark* with pride, saying no other man could boast that they had ever been marred for a greater cause, save the *saints* themselves.

There was collective amnesia where her past was concerned: because she would not tell, or claimed to have forgotten, it did not exist in the minds of those around her. Her slate was *clean.* I on the other hand, I was never to benefit from such generous clemency; my past followed me as if I too had it written on my arms - a stain no soap could cleanse.

When I was a boy, Mary Menham taught Sunday School; a strict matron, a Victorian throwback, but not unkind. I can't remember but perhaps I was causing disruption, for reluctantly my mother offered me the choice of continuing to attend, or staying home with my Father. I know she regretted her decision and blamed it for my moral decline. Not long after Abigail also withdrew citing irrevocable differences with *The Church*, and my Father believed this was the root cause of her own carnal indiscretions to come. My parents retained a friendship with Mrs Menham throughout the years that followed, and she paid her respects when they passed away...

She had been missing from church for several weeks, and although she was seen by her neighbours, she withdrew and did not answer the door or venture out. Then one night she arrived at the Priest's gate, asking for him. Catherine was reluctant at the lateness of the hour, but the old woman weaselled her way in. Fr Cotton was in the kitchen, he glanced up at her as she entered and knew instinctively that something was amiss, could feel the alarm bells being rung by his *spirit* within. She grabbed a steak knife from the counter, catching him on the forearm with a nasty gash. Catherine grabbed the woman by her *offending* hand, digging in her nails and teeth. Mary dropped the blade. She swung and smacked Catherine across the cheek, with force enough to topple her back against the wall clattering to the floor - blood trickled from her nose, her face stung, eyes involuntarily weeping. Cotton went in like a middleweight, landing combination body shots and uppercuts, *tasty* with his fists. The old lady was stronger but Cotton had the skill, driving her into retreat. Backed up against the kitchen door, as if she were *on the ropes*, Fr Cotton tried to seize the initiative. He unloaded with a hail of left right-left right hammer blows, pinning her in the storm. She was solid, powerful, her small frame unnaturally resistant to his fists. He tired, became ragged, threw wild hooks hopelessly at her head. Punched out, she picked him up and threw him across the room hard into the sink, breaking the unit from the wall; torn pipes gushed water, upturned dishes clattered...

Catherine's ears wrenched for what had befallen, his silence *Roared,* she screamed at his defeat. The old hag came in close to finish off his prostrate figure, and as she leant down he clocked her bull's-eye with a heavy *skillet.* Springing to his feet he bludgeoned her again and again and again, until she squirmed incoherent at his feet. Though winded and unsteady, he dragged her by the legs out of the kitchen, down the hall, on into the chamber separating his quarters from the church, and into the *forbidden room,* trailing a slug like residue. He unlocked the hatch to the basement, and dropped her rattling down the spiral staircase into the blackness of the *pit...*

He comforted a *bruised and shaken* Catherine until we arrived, responding to his sudden call. The thing down below beat against the hatch, ringing a pulsating clank, and spat forth hideous inhuman tones. His Blind Angel was hysterical, flinching with each subterranean beat. Fr Cotton held her as we fed her neat Gin to calm her nerves, which she spluttered down, and craved more to dull the *anguish.*

The banging ceased abruptly, as if she knew we were coming. Sean and I armed ourselves from the tool shed. Fr Cotton liberated his Holy Brand and Bone Mallet from the strong box in his study: the *Hammer and the Glory* he christened them with fondness. And from this his war-chest, from a box inside a box, he breathed life into Fr Albertine's old revolver...

We gathered round the shaft. I nervously unlocked the hatch, signalled the Priest, and lifted the lid; at once he splashed *holy water* down the hole into the blackness. The thing screeched scolded. Sean flipped the light switch for the cavern below, the sudden brightness startled her eyes and we saw her shrink away from the staircase. Fr Cotton descended the iron spiral at speed, Sean quick after him and I clumsily bringing up the rear, catching my boots on the steps. The Priest held his brand by the base of the Cross-bracing the long shaft hilt down his arm as a shield, parrying her blows and weighing in with his *mallet*. Sean joined, driving her back with his *hoe*. Overwhelmed by our onslaught she was overcome. Leaning on their weapons they pinned her down, and I bound her with *wire and rope*.

We tied her to the great monolith chair in the centre. Fr Cotton unlocked the cabinets that housed his many implements of persuasion, and we set to work, intent on eradicating the evil to free the woman beneath. For three days we plied her. The Priest exhausted every word and *spell* he could muster. We branded and we scorched her with blessed water and oil. In desperation we fired up the chair and sent *lightening* volts through her sinews and bones. But still the Wicked spirit would not budge to relinquish it's strangle-hold on poor Mary's *hide*. Each day she withered, emaciated by the curse, her skin fell from her wrinkles as if infected with a wasting disease. As each layer peeled the stench exposed an older rotting bouquet. Only her screams punctuated her cackles and blasphemous taunts; and every time she shrieked, Catherine cried out above.

Although we were out of sight, she seemed aware of our every deed; as we turned the screws on our captive, our *blind angel* suffered every wince, tormented by the necessary cruels of our daily war.

She cowered in her bedroom, deranged, without food or drink, regressing to some untold terror. She could not be counselled or offered comfort. When Fr Cotton found fresh cuts upon her arms he asked Sean to take her away, but she wouldn't, suffering panic attack and clawing at any who came within reach. In desperation The Priest descended into the pit, to *finish it* once and for all.

The figure may have been disintegrating in the chair: an image of the *living dead* rising from the grave, but the evil will coiled inside with bitterness was undefeated. The Holy Man had reached his plateau. He pulled the Revolver from his belt and pressed it point blank against the old woman's skull.

'Listen to me you Stupid Bitch! I'm gonna to say this only once: you let her go, or I'm gonna *mess* you up, with a bullet in your Dumb-Fat-Twisted-Brain! If you don't believe me,' he cocked the hammer, 'then you can take it up with me in the afterlife'.

He forced the barrel against her cranium pushing her head back in strain.

'No..!' the woman squealed in her own voice. 'Please, don't kill me, she's gone. Help me!' she pleaded.

Fr Cotton took a step back and the woman flopped her head forward in relief. But he looked unmoved.

'Ok Mrs Menham, if you're back, then you can pray for your soul,' the old woman met his eye, 'Pray with me Mary... You remember how to pray don't you?'

Her look narrowed, not betraying her but casting a doubt in my mind. Fr Cotton had wrestled back control, with the power of the *gun*, but I was on tenterhooks as to where he was going to take it.

'Mary Mary repeat after me: Our Father in Heaven, hallowed be your name...'

She didn't flicker, eyes sternly upon the Priest.

'Mary! Say the words: your kingdom come, your will be done...'

Her face became mean and spiteful, her silence *bellowed...* The Priest stepped back into her again, pressing the Black steel weapon against her forehead.

'On earth as in Heaven… If there is one ounce of you still left in there speak now, Before I send this Witch back to Hell!'

The creature opened her mouth to speak, but nothing came, there was no scrap of Mary Menham left. Resigned, the creature closed her eyes and Fr Cotton blew her away... and then finished his prayer.

Sean and I were, as usual, lumbered with the *burning and burying* of the unfortunate carcass. We always disposed of the remains on the skirts of the city dump, or, as in this case, scattered around the quarry - *skulduggery* in the wee hours.

Fr Cotton and Catherine slipped back into their domestic arrangement without ill effect, but we were extra careful around her, keeping the jeopardy and casualties of our war from her ears.

Whatever sin she may have chosen in her past, whatever was done unto her and befell - I am in no fit state to *judge.* I may be jealous of her time with the Priest, or jealous of the Priest with her; but none of it matters, not my feelings at least. All that matters is that he has someone to return home to, someone waiting at the end of each day of his *trial*; someone to cook his meal and stoke the fire, someone to ply her bow and sing a soulful *calm* over his troubles. I can only imagine how *solitary* his life was before, he is a lone soldier, but there's no need for him be *alone* in the long hours between the fight...

Catherine's loyalty to the Priest is unquenchable, for his protection and kindness she is forever *bound*; but if the *Devil* himself returns for her crimes, she knows that even Fr Cotton will have to yield...

And whosoever shall scandalize one of these little ones that believe in me: it were better for him that a millstone were hanged about his neck and he were cast into the sea.
Mark 9: 41
Douay-Rheims Bible

THE FATHER COTTON CHRONICLES: V

NIGHT OF THE HUNTED

...I will destroy man whom I have created from the face of the earth; both man, and beast, and the creeping thing, and the fowls of the air; for it repenteth me that I have made them. And, behold, I, even I, do bring a flood of waters upon the earth...
Genesis 6: 7, 17
King James Version

It was late one night when Catherine answered a call from the widow Mavis Brown's son Daniel. He informed her that his mother was *fading* and wouldn't last the night. Her health had deteriorated since her beloved husband Thomas had passed away, in increments imperceivable to those who tended her daily, but to Fr Cotton, who visited weekly without fail, a marked disintegration was apparent. She was close to the Priest, devout and loyal, and he had been of great support to her in her Grief. So once Catherine roused him from his warranted rest, he set out without delay to brave the Bitter Storm. His blind companion gave him a reproachful look, disapproving of the hour, and the baying weather-front, and not wishing him to leave her. Even if it hadn't been too wet for his pushbike, the *death-trap* was, as usual, up on end and kaput in her precious kitchen. Too late for public transport, and too miserly for a cab, he ventured out on foot.

A third day's drizzle flourished unabated, the streets were desolate and cold, blackened by the unremitting downpour. Accustomed to *nocturnal* exploration, midnight jaunts being a familiar part of his vocation, the *dark hours* held no fear. He weaved the back alleys and side streets, dangling his black bag by his side, staving off the chill with heavy cloak and under the protection of his trusty umbrella. His short-cut ran via the playground - the slide, swings and roundabout *ghostly* in their unoccupied state; the tip-tap pitter-patter of rainfall against the plastics and metals chimed as an orchestra of percussive instruments. While he attended the sick and the dying the civilised slept untroubled in their boxes, guilt free, as is their want. But even those who avoid holy worship tend to beckon the holy men when the *death bandit creeps* - the morbid side of his day job, but to him as everyday as the postman... Often, in the past, when he lived alone, and in the wee hours unable to rest his mind and sleep, he would set out to *grind* his concerns underfoot and feel closer to his people, observing their haunts and rush-hour districts without *witness*, scrutinizing their monuments from the vantage point of the *outsider.*

On past the School he rejoined the suburban street maze twisting and turning towards his destination... Sense by sense he gradually became aware of a lurking presence - the click of a footpad out of time to his steps and the rhythm of the rainfall, Goosebumps on his arms, and a prickling on the back of his neck as though the very atmosphere was *charged*. In the reflection of a parked car he made out two shapes hugging the shadows, darting in and out, closing in. No matter how hard he tried not to give himself away, he couldn't help but quicken his pace. At the junction, a third made his presence felt; no longer concealed they drove him on into their trap. Two more creatures guarded the road ahead. Five-to-one they closed, trying to corral him into the *underpass*; he knew they would not be alone - others would be waiting unseen on the other side. They each but one wore yellow rain-macks, length down to their knees, yoke coloured and shimmering with rain, hoods pulled over their heads. The odd man out wore a peppered grey raincoat and polished shoes, features traced under his big black wing-span umbrella, oozing calm and calculating intent. These men were under no possession, but were *evil* of their own will; hungry for it, thirsty for wrong...

The Priest looked deep into the *grave - death* waited inside, the dark wet tunnel was no place to die; there'd be no way out alive. A desperate standoff loitered, as the rain tambourined off the bonnets and rooftops, ticking out his remaining time... He made a *sudden dash* between the vehicles, traversing the barrier onto the main road, dropping his umbrella in the clamber. They pursued; from the other side three more foot soldiers emerged from cover. The pack encircled the Holy man on the central line, the road empty of traffic, not a solitary car or distant headlight. They ripped out the cables and broke the lamps illuminating the isolation of tarmac. Now afforded an arena of seclusion, the creatures began to encroach, advancing with painstaking spite - man shape, yet hunkered down, paddling on all fours, long arms and spider-like fingers stretching forth tasting the air; *Growling, Barking, Baring* their teeth - oversized, or in mouths consisting of too many, which he couldn't tell.

Clawing and *reaping* one reared up, Fr Cotton drew aside his cloak, and a *silver flash* in the night he withdrew his weapon from the concealment of its scabbard. With upward stroke he split a gash in his attacker from navel to nose - it fell listless and didn't rise again... He spun brandishing *his Bayonet*, swirling poised to strike, improvising his bag as a shield protecting his flank. His assailants, who'd been eager and boastful now thought twice, screening their fear in howls of *bravado* and snarling aggression.

The Priest demonstrated his swordsmanesque prowess with his Dancing blade and *barked* back, 'Come on you *Filthy* Mutts, let's finish this like men... Stand up and show me your *Bellies!* Playing at Bitches doesn't scare me' *(though he was indeed afraid)...*

The headlights of a lone car manifested in the distance; the creatures hesitated, debating telepathically if they could risk an assault in time; deciding against it they scattered as the beams of the vehicle bore down. Fr Cotton frantically gestured for the car to stop, forgetting his rapier. The driver, his headlights penetrating the unlit carriageway, confronted by a man, weapon in hand and body *splayed* at his feet, accelerated onto the wrong side of the road to avoid the incident, and sped by... The Priest, taking advantage of the chance interruption, ran following the road, heading towards civilization, keeping to the light.

They seemed not to pursue, but he knew better; they would be vying to head him off, and although he could not spot a scout, he knew one would be shadowing. At the late hour he knew all would be closed to him, doors locked and inaccessible; but the station would be open, he could seek refuge there, if he could make it...

The mirrored Office Blocks grew floor by floor in status, and *fallout-grey* Multi-Storey Parking structures lumbered alongside - inhospitable concrete prisons. The ground vibrated stalks of innumerable droplets, all surfaces shimmered in grades of liquid monochrome; even the litter bins overflowed, resembling decorative garden fountains at regular intervals along the avenue. Iron grates prohibited entry to the arcades and scattering of shops. From time to time in self-consciously futile gestures, he hammered on offices, thinking he might rouse a hapless security guard, and waved in distress at surveillance cameras sentinelled high above the main street - *a shipwrecked soul* flagging down a passing ship on the far horizon.

And then he caught sight of himself reflected in the *dark pane* of a storefront. Absentmindedly he still carried the *murdering blade* in hand - a stone cold *killer* echoed back at him. He sheathed the weapon, and recalled the day to his mind when Fr Albertine had handed him the instrument with noble reverence. A sword *victorious* of many battles in the hand of his renowned mentor, and in the hand of the old Priest's grandfather: Parmellor. A career soldier of Anglo-Indian lineage, he had served protecting the boarders of his colonial homeland, and then the Southern hills of Africa. But none of his training or experience in the field could prepare him for the inglorious *folly* of the Western Front, and the Ypres-Passchendaele campaign.

The tactical bombardment tore up the land, drainage canals

were rendered obsolete, and unseasonably heavy rain turned the terrain into an impassible sea of *liquid mud* and water-filled shell-craters. The trees were *blunted* to trunks, branches and leaves torn away. Duckboards were laid across the newly forged swamps; men under heavy burden would slip off the path into the craters and *be gone*. Even the new tanks and heavy mechanisms of war were bogged down and defeated. …Most every name he knew was lost to the shelling, or the heavy guns, the quickening mud, or the rancorous gas. Shell shock was common as *lice* and necessary as tobacco.

His grandfather confided that during his nights at the front, he was haunted by the memory of a stranded horse, its back legs tangled in barbed wire, front legs stuck in a shell hole of coagulating mud, dying to hold its head above the mire. He said the image summed up the *Big Bloody Conflict* - a trapped creature: the more it fought against itself the more *engraved* it became; and worse still - the more it kicked and bayed the more unlikely an onlooker to risk hurt to intervene. So Parmellor watched it exhaust, and succumb, troubling him at the time more than any human casualty. *Flaring nostrils* and sopping mane, great *teeth* spraining far beyond lips - and the *screams*, if that's what you call them, the despair emanating from the thrashing sludge-caked head swimming above its inevitable grave. The mud drying about its *feverish* skin transformed to ashen grey and cracked around its eyes - as it was graven in stone... It was only after the grand conflict was over, and settled in an English home, that he allowed himself to remember the men *he left behind.* He was as big and brave as they come, but those bloody faces *hounded* him for the remainder of his life.

His Father was as reticent about his Second War exploits and his Grandfather was generous. Parmellor told August Albertine when only a boy that War was not about Glory, or Victory, but about *Killing* - while in the other ear his Father told him it was

Honorable, the making of a man, and to serve was expected of him as the family tradition. His grandfather spoke of a time where the waters subsided, though not entirely, only enough to excavate the partial remains of those departed: piles of half submerged arms and faces welling in each furrow and crater. The German's were dug in deep, but in a rare offensive his *trench* was cascaded by heavy mortar fire, weakening their resilience. They were utterly defeated, cut off, killed or buried. The sky was dense with ash, smoke and vapor - a dirty blanket overpowering the fading grains of daylight. From out of this their enemy came, Stormtroupers, gasmask clad anonymous. Although the opposing force was small, they were highly trained veterans and held the surprise advantage. The last few able men were easily overrun. Parmellor found himself camouflaged under mudslide and fallen comrades. The Troopers killed the wounded - robotically fulfilling their task, refraining from loosening a shot, knife and bayonet sufficient enough. An enemy came in close jabbing into the prone bodies, slashing randomly into the pile, making sure of death. One lunge pierced Parmellor's upper thigh. He stifled a *cry*.

The officer ordered his men to scout and secure the perimeter, while he searched and robbed the bodies of their cigarettes and trinkets, though for the most part found only their treasured photographs and letters from home. Far more thorough than his men, he cut away bags and clothes with his broad unmounted bayonet. Over Parmellor he tore at the burying bodies and then tossed them aside. There would be no *playing dead* - his *life* would be discovered. He dared not close his eyes and onset defenselessness, and only hoped the officer would take his *pupils* for silent. The German yanked him this way and that pulling at his pockets, and only in frustration did he look up to the face. The officer caught his eye and turned immediately pale with fright - in the nick of time Parmellor thrust his fingers into his enemy's mouth to suppress the *alarm*. The officer bit down hard, Parmellor grasped the blade from his adversaries disbelieving hand and *slit* his throat. He pushed the gargling body away down into the death-pile and buried himself deep into the muddy bank of earth... The yells of the Troopers when they came were dim to his ears; he couldn't gamble on *trusting* a breath. They set off grenades in retaliation, he was unearthed and buried again, and a long darkness of *ugly* dreams followed.

...In the early morn his countrymen retook the lost ground without resistance, but by-past the *ruins* for dead, and they were, except for Parmellor, who crawled from the pit peppered with shrapnel and limping wounds, and unwilling to be parted from his Officer's *trophy*.

Fr Cotton reached the station unmolested, except for the probing fingers of the rain, the crackling wind about his ears, the hoarse rattle of his breath, and the consequences of his tremolo heartbeat. He thought he had befallen another trap when he discriminated shadows lurking to the pillars of the entrance, only to discover they were working women unappreciated on a bleak night.

The friction of his wet fabric and the flap of his footfalls echoed conspicuous in the lofty chamber. The floor wore the unfavourable perfume of cleaning fluid, and yet the stench of urine lingered on in the *bitter* aftertaste. The essence of vomit clung to corners disguised as limescale, not unlike the drunks and tramps *secreted* on benches, masquerading as the living, sheltering from the unfriendly sky.

The illusory safety of the light drew him over to the Grand Centrepiece Clock, pointing black decorative fingers with ominous certainty; the timepiece, the footbridge and the Dome, the only original remnants of the station's early 20th Century design. Arrival/departure boards clattered through their programmes, a background reminder of the *pressing* of time. He debated his choices with the voice inside his shell - he could try to hold out 'till morning, hunkering down with the homeless, or descend to the underground and keep out of sight; or he could cross the bridge to the outer platforms and try to loose himself in the crowd of the next arrival... Two figures stole in through the entrance. He tentatively stepped towards the underground, but another shape floated up the escalator...

He made for the footbridge - two more of the yellow consortium advanced across from the other side. Trapped in a narrow pass, he liberated a tiny bottle from his bag and splashed his nearest adversary in the *face*. The holy water had no adverse effect, the victim laughed mocking. Rattled, Fr Cotton drew his weapon and challenged them.

'Come on then... Come on! ...COME ON!'

They collectively reached out their hands, leaning over one another in a wave of *clasping, groping tentacles* that inched closer: long teeth in the *jaws* of unwanted attention.

'Come on... Destroy ME..! Destroy me... if you *dare!*
Sed et si ambulavero in *valle mortis...* I-will-fear-no-Evil…!'

Fingers latched onto his bag and he was drawn into a tug of war. The threat of his blade kept the others at bay. The bag sprang open, fabric torn, his bottles and sick communion set deserting… He let go - the tugging hands fell back in a tangle of bodies and limbs. Swiveling towards the outstretched arms preventing his escape, he let fly at the nearest villain with his sharpened *savior,* removing the fingers of one outstretched hand and following through to the wrist of the other, so it *flapped* back on a ragged piece of skin. The creature fell to his knees - face frozen in *soundless scream.* The other adversary grabbed Fr Cotton's arms; unable to swing he kicked the foe between the legs. His opponent clung on, so the Priest braced him on his shoulder and tipped him over the railing down onto the tracks below.

Regaining their senses, those behind scrambled to stand and drove at him. The Priest swung over the edge and let himself drop down onto the 2nd platform. His fallen adversary hobbled in discomfort down in the valley of the tracks, blood trickling out of his hood from a concealed head wound. Fr Cotton ran through the archway onto platform three, jumped down onto the tracks and ran out of the station and into the *night*...

Fr Albertine awoke from trouble and restlessness to find *something,* something he wouldn't confide in me, not back then; I had much to learn before he would divulge such secrets and purpose. What he saw was a scrawny teenage *Girl* shielding a candle in her hand, dancing patterns of flame marbling across her *olive* skin, smoldering in her *deep autumn* eyes... He sat up with a start but she was gone, *as if never there*... The smoke of an extinguished wick corrosive to his nostrils. He rose and switched on the light. A candle from his private alter trailed a tapering wisp.

Somehow he understood this was a signal that Fr Cotton was in direr need, he felt it whispering in his bones, and no longer questioned the origin of the apparition.

He raised the alarm, summoning Sean and I to the church where he *interrogated* Catherine. We set off with haste for the home of Mavis Brown... It lay in darkness, door on the latch; we could rouse no light from the unresponsive switches. Luckily we had brought torches to cut clearly through the heavy drapes of *deathly* nightshade - wobbling moon-disks picking out craters of detail and throwing creepy ink shadows on the walls. The stink of charged meat and pulpy bubbling wafted from the long simmering pot and frying pan. The radio caught dead air - tuned to the frequency of the *dammed.*

We found her several days deceased, neglected, and the pained trial of her departure graven dramatically into her expression. We stumbled upon her son, a fresh kill, floating in a pool of his own *blood* on the kitchen floor, as the washing machine spun and spun.

The old Tower Block jutted up from the earth, *grey* in the daylight, *dusty* silver in the *dusken* rain, looming above the emaciated *apocalyptic* trees in its wake. Notorious and ugly, a *slum* on stilts; more windows were boarded up than paned, a patchwork gradually climbing the edifice like *poverties* ivy. He feared the security intercom would prevent his entry, but found the heavy door broken ajar - *ram-raided* by the progeny of social-deprivation, indirectly handing him grace. He pressed for the elevator. A delayed groan indicated life in the mechanism, but the display was dead, no clue to from which floor it descended.

He felt the presence of the *unholy soldiers* closing in. He debated the stairs, but knew they would only slow him down. The elevator rattled like a bucket freefalling down a well, yet was still taking an *age* to reach the ground floor. The *beasts* collected just beyond the crippled door, he could see their cloaks incandescent in the entrance light, rendered in liquid metal and crawling *alive* with worms of rain. He faced them: his fingers *tingled,* his quick breaths shallow, lightheaded, weakened with *fear.* One of the yellow figures entered, squeezing through the aperture. In slow motion to the Priest's adrenaline pumped veins, the fellow exposed his thorny-nailed hands to pull back the hood from his smooth *ivory* domed head - his poise was steady, controlled, but his eyes were *wild* with *sadistic* intent. He opened his vicious mouth as wide as he could, wider than should be *natural,* and displayed his weapons in a *silent roar...*

Forgotten, the elevator door he was backed up against opened and Fr Cotton teetered back on his heels into the container. Regaining his wits he banged the ball of his fist repeatedly against the panel-buttons. The man-creature was too slow to react, his brethren swamped through the *mangled* entrance and he lurched aggressively towards the Priest. The door snapped shut with hostility, no more sophisticated than an archaic toaster. One solid thump followed as the creature vented its discontent.

The elevator was hauled like an anchor, clunking chain and dead weight, as sluggish as if the mass of the sea were a resist. He feared the ascent was so pitiful that his assailants would likely overtake, and be waiting when the curtains opened for the show to begin. He pressed the 12th floor button repeatedly in frustration, hoping the height would slow them down. A chilling *draft* penetrated the steel shell from some hidden design flaw, but didn't stir the *stagnant* air. He strained vainly to calculate, but couldn't find a way to distinguish the passing of each floor.

The elevator crunched to a premature halt, he instinctively knew he wasn't at the summit. The door opened screeching metal. The landing was still - no whispers or footfalls. Graffiti adorned the wall ahead - layers of names, tags and obscenities each vying to outdo the last. He didn't dare peep out into the vacuous tunnel. He pressed forcefully on the top button expectant of a sudden lunge into his cage. A small part of him deliberated whether to dart out and hide on the uninfected floor, but as he formed his plan the door clamped shut and the machine resumed its slow ascent.

A thought had taken root. If they could make it to the top, they'd corner him, but if he got off at 11 he might escape. If they weren't all the way up, then they'd be on his heels, but he decided to risk it and hammered on the button not even knowing if the malfunctioning contraption would avail him.

This time when the elevator came to a rest he bolted out gambling on his luck or willing to take them head on, risking the dim and unloving corridor, charging into the claustrophobia until he burst out onto the stairwell. He was, as he hoped, below the top floor. The *square spiral* geometrically descended, a gaping hole at its centre. No sign of foe, he made a dash for it, swiftly downhill. The ruckus alerted his *enemies*; they burst out of the doors of the upper floor. He chanced a fleeting look up, three of them were on his trail; his efforts had gained a two floor head start.

The shaft was lit intermittedly (by vandalism rather than design) a *collage* of lights and darks, making it hazardous to gauge his footfalls on the shadow steps, and obscuring the very *bottom* of the *steep well*. Immense puddles collected the strands of rain stealing in, and rapids poured waterfalling down the stairs, and over the edge into the abyssful fall - an audible reminder of the scope of the *precipice*.

He felt his pursuers closing, narrowing his advantage… And then he perceived figures beneath ascending from the lower floors; he was trapped between the *hammer and the anvil*. Each of these parties could now see the other as they circled the spiral. The pack above spurred on by the anticipation of the flytrap, closed in rapidly, at his heels. He detected one below lagging behind, no doubt the dog he had *capsized* back in the station, his companion though would be on him fast.

Almost in their clutches, he took drastic action. In full stride he hurdled onto the feeble rail and leapt with true daring across the *chasm*… In mid-air he felt alive with death: heavy with dead weight, no breath or heat beat, *ash* in his veins, staring into the deep bottomless *void*, timeless in the *wake* of a black hole, existing both in time and outside of it - looking back at himself suspended… And then like a *cannonball* he clattered with *direct atrocity* down onto the level below - his timing impeccable, impacting into his slow hobbling assailant with thunder, using the other man to break his fall…

The *straggler* was broken against the wall; Fr Cotton stumbled away from the wreckage, unsteady, tripping down a flight of steps tearing at his hands and knees as he came to an abrupt stop. Fighting a stiffness as *potent* as rigor-mortis, and a drum and base head - he drove on down, fleeing the hot pursuit of his enemies…

The gapping chasm kept flashing before his eyes, aggravated by the looming darkness at the base of the well. He splashed off the bottom step into a cold reservoir of pooled rain, slipping ungainly into the shallow bay. The outline of light presented the exit and he bundled through the doors on into the entrance from where he had begun.

He expected *Others* there waiting to hamper his escape, where they were he did not know. He suffered, reeling from his toil, had pressing need to slow his antagonists. Acting quickly he unshackled his army blade and positioned to the side of the door. He heard the splash of his hunters and as the first burst through from the dark into the stark light, he *hacked* him between his neck and shoulder with a powerful downward stroke, and kicked him back to withdraw the savage bayonet. The figure blocked the door as his shocked hands gripped at the *angry wound,* blood pumped *unrestricted* through his fingers, a *fountain* of red over yellow.

The Priest turned and ran best he could out of the monolith Tower…

He aimed for the nearby park, hoping to lose them in the darken seclusion… The hedges and treeline offered camouflage but no defense. He made for the long slanting field that ran abreast to a modest lake. Lit only by lamps arrayed around the perimeter, the central expanse was a hive of picnics and ball games in daylight, now dense with the absence of life or illumination; he was a sailor in a fog bound sea, to the scant eye no different that any other tree in the forest - equally disadvantaged as the seasoned hunter.

This was it - he redrew his blade and awaited the Alamo… The rainfall deepened, falling austerely vertical and mean, hampering his vision, and laying weight upon his shoulders. He spoke a quiet word of prayer, 'Lord, do not forsake me in my hour of need!'

His foes discarded their raincoats, and crawled on all fours, *naked as dogs.* The blades of grass harboured a river of droplets, and it was the disturbance of these alone against their bodies that betrayed their circling movement. He held his bayonet blade out in the downpour - as slippery silver as the rain that broke upon its bow.

Two of his adversaries attacked as one, simultaneously tempting his steel and engaging his flank; Fr Cotton anticipated, parried, and latched to grab hold of a flailing limb - smooth and slippery wet, it slid through his fingers and vanished out of sight as quickly as they came... The focal of the hurricane, he beat a skip faster; resisting panic he endeavored to place himself in the laping waves of a peaceful shore, and regain a token of calm...

Bounding *full pelt* on all fours out of the *glassy veil,* one of the pack charged headlong and hit him like a freight train. The impact sent them spinning away counter to one another - two cars in the *aftershock* of a high speed wreck, tossing Cotton off his feet to land on his back in the drench. The Dog-man on him quicker than he could recover, pinned Fr Cotton's blade wielding hand to the dirt by the wrist, digging in his filed to a point nails. With his spare hand he grabbed the Priest by the throat, leveraging down with all his might, an expression of outlandish *murder* corrupting his features. Fr Cotton gouged at his attacker's eye until it weakened its hold - he lunged up with his sliver of steel and *gutted* his unwanted companion. The Priest heaved the body over, his legs and midriff bathed in his opponents *stain*; his own blood ran diluted from his scuffed neck and arm, washing in the storm.

With the Holy Man *floored* his opponents narrowed. As one loomed over him he scrambled to his knees and wielding his gladius blade two-handed for maximum effect, he slashed his target across his exposed thigh. The figure dropped like a bird without wing - Fr Cotton grabbed at his lame leg. The Dog-man fought to clamber away, like a wildebeest from the clutches of *crocodile* jaws, thrashing in the wet of the lawn. The Priest held his silvering sheen aloft, almost hanging in the non-existent wind as the sail on a *Cutter*... And then he brought it down with ferocious cruelty, not once but *thrice*, until the exposed man, smooth as marble, lay face down, unmoving in the mud and the blood and the *heavenly tears*.

Fr Cotton kneeled on the battle field, painted in liquefied earth and wine from the unholy cup. The slick bodies of his victims were inscribed with text and detail, though illegible and obscured by layers of watery tea brown and blood black as oil in the night. His last two opponents withdrew deep into the rain-choked shade. He waited, and waited, but no sigh or sound of them returned. Weary, hurting, and soaked to the skin, he stood and surveyed the carnage one last time, with leaden heart... And then set out for home, walking slow steps in the mire, each footfall more laboured than the last.

The outer gate dwelled clear of a dip in the field and up the gravel pathway. The cluster of lights at the bottleneck entrance sparkled the rain afire in orange and golds. He felt safer drawing to the illumination ahead, for he had feared this was where they would make their final assault... As the lawn basined the waters drained towards the rut, filling the ground thick with arduous mud. The curve of the pathway ran flooded as a stream, feeding all the gathering waters down into the overflowing lake. *Eerie* in deathly grey, the surface was impenetrable to the eye. The *Island* where wildfowl usually sheltered under tree, lay submerged, bare branches sticking up from the centre, Atlantis succumbing to the great flood. The perimeter fence, child high for safety, also lifted its head above the *false* tide, the uncertain line of a miniature viaduct dancing across the surface.

His feet stuck, bogged down in the murking soil, as if shoed in boots of laden *gravity*. As he yanked himself free, one foot sprang from its leather and he fell ungracefully face down in the quagmire, jarring his shoulder. The surface was a flow, and as he wriggled, maneuvering to right himself, eel-like he began to slip, gradually at first, and then *helplessly* gathering pace down the mud bank into the rushing furrow of the pathway. He was carried down the waterslide, and no amount of jostling or agility could prevent his *ride* into the lake.

It was only an abrupt collision with the perimeter fence that interrupted his decent into the heart of the *dark water.* The impact against the painted but rusting iron pulled him under, and stole the silver blade from his grasp; his limbs tangled in the railings momentarily, but then he utilized the vertical bars and hauled his head out - coughing and spluttering.

Thought the downpour suffered a temporary lull, the chilly waters ground at his bones. He strove to wade himself out of the overflow, but weary the rolling waters cajoled him back against the fence. He breathed deeply, hating and loving the *iron line* that held him. Looking up the rivering walkway towards the gate, scheming for an escape route from the insurmountable obstacle, he beheld the last two mercenaries approaching from the distance, careful to avoid his mistake, standing tall and straight, *naked as the moon*; adorned with unholy tribal scaring, tattoo-like shapes acid etched through their *flesh.* Trapped, Fr Cotton lusted for the fallen blade; desperately he reached down into the bitter cold and fished for his only hope.

He labored to reach the bottom without submerging. Looking back over his shoulder, the two men had gained ground, but cautiousness was delaying their advance. He held his breath and immersed into the shivering water. He ran his hand through the shallow depths, all manner of refuse was clogged against the fence: jagged cans and bottles, gravel and sticks - he knew it was harsh against his fingers but numbness spared the nicks and the pain.

He broke the surface gasping for fresh breath, a great turmoil drew him fast, and he spun to find one of the wicked foes almost on him, careening down the waterway into the overflow, his associate not far behind. The Dog-man went for him, Fr Cotton tried to dodge aside but the water dragged him slow. The aggressor tagged him with clawish nails as he bundled past hard into the railings - the Holy Man flinched, enduring lacerations to his torso. Knowing the second man would be on him imminent, The Priest rallied, he scored a keen punch before his first aggressor could find his feet, and pressing his knee under the man's chin, he submerged his assailant below the *unforgiving waters.*

The second man hit forcefully, piling Cotton against the iron rail, but he held his victim firmly gripped. This new attacker seized hold and dug its teeth into his back - a *pain* surpassing any numbness he felt, penetrating to his *core* (a sensation he would not quickly forget). He strove to shake him but the bear-hug wouldn't give. The Priest released his now stagnant bundle, twisted and pressed his remaining enemy against the fence, sandwiched between himself and the iron. If anything the villain drove in deeper with *nail and tooth*; Fr Cotton called out in agony, unable to contain the hate. Grabbing the fence behind he lent back until both their bodies were arcing over the boundary - until they both toppled over the rail head first into the lake. The bite released, Fr Cotton gripped the handrail, and as his opponent floundered to stand or swim he braced his attacker in headlock with his free arm. The Priest returned the favour and *bit* down on his nose, the man swore in distress. Fr Cotton released him and battered repeatedly point blank until his opponent was washed away and the Holy Man was lashing out at water alone. He watched the body float towards the hidden isle, bobbing in and out of the black-liquid, not knowing if the fiend was unconscious or dead. He held onto the fence and dared not follow. His other victim he could not see, and was perhaps also lost to the *watery grave.*

His slow climb from the gutter was greater than any trial his opponents could collectively muster, as he was repeatedly driven back to where he'd begun. Many times he *despaired,* and many times he *prayed,* but *once* he climbed the mountain to the Gate.

After searching the entire city it seemed, we found him disabled by exhaustion, not two blocks from his home. We returned him to Catherine, and had Dr Balsom, a man sympathetic to our needs, attend his hurts. Once recovered he told us he had encountered their leader; he had been waiting for him, sitting casually at the bus stop, swinging his legs to pass the time. He rose as Fr Cotton approached, opening his umbrella, as if the shower was more of an inconvenience than the loss of his troops. He smiled, though his true intent was unreadable, gave a slight nod, crossed the road and vanished back into the bands of grey…

By morning the skies were clear, the rain having passed far from harm. While Fr Cotton recuperated under Catherine's watchful care, Fr Albertine wasted no time and scoured the lake, under the pretence of searching for mislaid bodies, though in reality he hunted for his grandfather's prize. For three days he waded as the overflow receded around him. He unearthed no sign or victim from the skirmish, but his precious relic found its way back to his *hand,* and the relay continued unbroken…

…I am going to put an end to all people, for the earth is filled with violence because of them. I am surely going to destroy both them and the earth.
Genesis 6: 13
New International Version

THE FATHER COTTON CHRONICLES: VI
THE GYPSY

*And the sea gave up the dead that were in it: and death and hell
gave up their dead that were in them. And they were judged, every
one according to their works.*
Revelation 20:13
Douay-Rheims Bible

Her *past* was a mystery - fragments of paper *littering* the
snow, as though she could bend her clairvoyancey in reverse,
cleansing the bygone as easily as she could unveil the to-come.
There is something unsettling about a *wandering* spirit who plants
roots, however shallow; whatever affair made her dwell, she locked
secretly out of sight, far from *harms way*. Yet her restless feet
would lead her astray without foreword - weeks falling from the
calendar and her journey's destination undisclosed. Rumor from
her inner circle was that she sought out new places, traveling in
disguise, so as to meet strange men with *anonymity*. She lived in an
area unkindly labeled 'Bohemian Row', a Mecca for like minded
peoples: poets, artists, writers, intellectuals and the like. From
here she *entertained*, practiced her *Gift*, and procured a band of
followers. That was the public face of things. What manipulations,
schemes and plots she strategized to barter the devotion of the
aristocratic and the influential, remained the currency of espionage
- information and secrets: patronage and protection…

   She would drip-feed Fr Cotton scraps of enigma, *scattershot*
clues, leading him to unearth all manner of wrongs. Occasionally
he was given to call on her, and I'd tag along, but I'd be excluded
and made to wait while he enjoyed a private audience. Fr Albertine
instructed me to chaperone, he did not trust her, and neither did I
- for no other reason than the prohibition derided me.

   'Shall I tell your Fortune Julian Boone?' She threatened to
read me, assigning misbehavior to the distrustful looks I'd given
her every time she'd led him away.

One day, to my lasting surprise, I received one of her personalized tarot cards and a message asking me to come alone… and strict instructions not to inform Fr Cotton. I considered it ill-advised to decline, or not show, even though my heart desired it. I had never visited unaccompanied, where I was the main course. An evening appointment found the row and her terrace less inviting. I climbed the dark entrance steps as if awaiting rough sentence. Her building, always bustling with life music and colour, was now dead and cold, save for the ghost of a warm light harboring far above. I pressed the grating buzzer and the door clicked. The polished glint of ornaments and mirrors punctuated the shade pulling my glance to unfriendly movements all my own. The trace of light drew me up the narrow stairwell.

As I came upon her sitting there, she seemed *vulnerable* for the first time to my witnesses, though confident in her choice. She was prepared as if I were a client: waiting at the table with the objects of her profession at hand.

'Make yourself comfortable Julian.'

I disliked her calling me a name that only my parents and teachers had uttered, it was contradictorily formal and intimate.

Her age was hard to judge: her dark-pupil eyes experienced, vibrant and impossible to read. She wore her crow-black hair tied up perched atop of her head, neatly businesslike, with strategic strands shooting down to accentuate her *neck* tantalizingly and show off her exquisite jaw line and *cheekbones*. Her voice deeper than the average woman, and soft, never shrill - pitched for *intimacy,* drawing all into her confidence web. Attractive: a common man's Ava Gardner; but with an air of otherness, as if she *resonated* on a different *frequency.*

The only evidence of corporeal weakness were her unshapely hands: long, all bone and spidely. Ironic that fingers used to spellbind so eloquently, skilled at dealing out the cards of fate, the envy of any harp musician, were indeed unlovely: it was as though she had been *cursed* to have the instrument of her enchantment *stricken* down with *woe*. Knowing this to be her flaw, she disguised her unsightly digits, flaunting in an endless array of slender and elegant gloves.

She tendered insignificant conversation, but lacked the temperament, and I was playing hard to get.

When things petered out I cut to it, 'Why am I here, what is it you want from me?'

She paused momentarily before broaching the subject, '... How much do you know about Vincent's past?'

Irritated, I responded in brief, 'I know all I need.'

'There are things about your friend that he has kept from you, some, some *fundamental* things... He has many hidden truths... and one *Great* Secret - an enviable chance of fate...' Though I was inclined to disbelieve, she ploughed on with compelling sincerity.

'*His* Kind don't easily walk the earth, they're too few and far between; the makings of a champion, born in the *cage* of ordinary skin, and undermined by the very *Institution* he serves' (*Spite* in her voice at the very thought of it).

'He has a gift and there are those who would supplant it, or pervert it to their own ends. ...I tell you this much because it is you and you alone who is in place to guide and protect his investment...

You have some skill Julian, a kind of your own, unrecognized by others. Most wouldn't trust you with a quest of worth; a man of disreputable past. But I trust you *Joon*... Don't you ask yourself *Why?* The answers are encrypted to the cards, and the cards do not lie...'

I looked suspiciously at the deal by her hand.

'Don't worry,' she smirked, ' these are not for you - not today... What's the point of *reading you* if you don't trust me? ...Albertine forewarned you. He is right to *Doubt* me, and don't deny it, I know he does. I have plans for Vincent, Glorious Plans! That he would not approve... I'll never win Albertine over, but you Julian, I will earn your trust. I will start by explaining why a virtuous man like He would have need of the services of a woman like me...'

She explained that when still only a boy his Mother took her own life. Placed her *head* in the *oven.* There was no need to leave a note, he knew why she did it, she had drummed it into him every day of his young life, through her words, and actions, subconscious and conscious - that he'd *ruined* her: if he hadn't come along she could have made something of herself. ...It's impossible to measure the *impact* on a child. Then something happened of equal *magnitude,* at least in the eggshell mind of the boy.

His Father inherited her *conceit,* not blaming her, but blaming the child for their *ruination.* He didn't like the boy hanging around the house, so he'd send him out to play. The young Vincent would wander the streets, come dark or rain. He was drawn to the bustle of the station, where he'd shelter and sit and watch and feel part of the world. One day through the coming and goings he saw a young woman, heavy red shawl about her head, features *immaculate,* calm in the *eye* of the storm, focused only on *him.* This was no ordinary woman: she was otherworldly, and she chose him, singling him out from the *ranks of the many.* The insubstantial world fettered pompous and insignificant - an inconsequential scurrying unawares of the true nature of things: the precarious dear *fragility* on which so much hung ...And then she was gone. But for those few moments his heart ceased to beat and was reborn - and the trajectory of his life was given to alter forever; unquestionable forging and molding an already impressionable and Motherless boy. What he really saw doesn't matter - his *Faith* was cemented...

He became drawn to a local tramp - bearded and sage-like. The young Vincent was unyielding in his conviction that this unkempt man was *The Baptist* returned to guide him. The Tramp, for whatever reason, took this lonesome boy under his wing and showed him what it took to *survive* on the street; taught him how to handle himself, and introduced him to all the saints hidden amongst the vagrants: Saint Francis, Rita of Cassia, and Bernadette, each one toiling for the good of mankind in the *misbegotten* undergrowth. They showed him places far from polite society, things a boy shouldn't have to see.

It was inevitable that the draw of the *clergy* snared him, though the Baptist was wise enough to instruct him to keep his *peculiar* ideas to himself. The Tramp's grounding kept him in good stead - never was he seduced away from the real people he was sent to serve. His study outwardly seemed untroubled, but steadily the *shadow of a threat* reappeared to haunt the young Priest... He'd scent the linger of his Mothers perfume when returning to his humble digs, and a *watchful* presence tailing his steps in the dark hours, and noises to restless his sleep. He kept his own council, and contrary to good advice, and against the code of his collar, he went to see *The Gypsy,* knowing her by reputation to be a woman discrete.

'I spoke with his Mothers voice,' the Gypsy affirmed, ' she was *Bitter, Insensitive.* Said she didn't hate *him* - it was the *child* she hated. The child she resented and blamed for her undoing... That was all she wanted to say, and didn't bother him again - but the words of her message *lingered long...*

I respected his *secret,* and as a confidant outside of the Judgment of the Church, he came back for *more,* and told me so many things... We became fast friends, and helped each other where we could. Though in other ways our collusion was of detriment to both our reputations; I certainly was not popular for engaging a Holy Man *here...*'

Fr Cotton was distracted, my absence *absent* from his thoughts. The day I engaged the *Gypsy* he attended the funeral of Fr Dowie, a Priest callously murdered in the grounds of his church by a man claiming to be Jesus, God and the Devil all rolled into one *repugnant* ball. With a history of mental illness, in and out of institutions all his young life, their was legitimate concern that the killer would forgo the judgment of prison, and in no time at all be released back into society to menace and slay.

Even before the ceremony he knew it would be his task to peel back the veneer and expose whether this young thug was mad, or, in fact, a *servant of the enemy.* And it seemed that the family had also been informed; reassured that their *Best Man* was on the job. As he paid his respects, the Sister and Niece confronted him at the graveside, in front of God and all. The grieving sibling clasped him firmly by the arm and stared her watery eyes straight into his.

'Don't let him get away with it… He knew what he was doing. He deserves to be behind bars for the rest of his miserable life - DON'T let him *fool* them!'

The Daughter steadied her shaking mother, and directed her frustration at the Priest. 'Make him *pay.* I have no forgiveness to give that-' she restrained her foul words.
'Get him. Do whatever you do. Whatever it takes.' She held back the temptation of tears, anger out-muscling loss, 'He was a Father to me… You are accountable to this family, to us, do you hear me… To *Us..!*'

What response could he give? He resisted the heartfelt temptation to promise them all they needed, wanted and commanded.

At the reception he was taken aside into private rooms by the Bishop and his network of influence. Surrounded by those of honorable importance, arrayed in their fine cloth, they looked down their noses at him, as if he were a toilet cleaner - But they needed someone to *stir the refuse,* and cleanse that which they would never risk the sullying of their manicured hands to be rid of. As predicted, they *requested* his services; they would not have invited him otherwise. He would be called to assess the spiritual needs of the misguided antagonist. It had been arranged. In fact the perpetrator had requested a holy confessor, from the incarceration of his rubber room. To deny him would be an infringement upon his *human rights,* even if he was a Priest Killing Degenerate…

Fr Cotton doubted he'd be able to ascertain his guilt - his kind are the most deceiving. Fr Albertine on the other hand could have *read* him in a microsecond, being a man hotwired with an infallible barometer.

'I am going to tell you a story that I need you to believe. I'm gonna tell you because *he never will…*' the Gypsy continued.

…She revealed that while still an unseasoned Priest, Fr Cotton was approached by an agitated couple imploring him to exorcise the *badness* from their home. As he experienced falling attendances and the faltering lure of the church, and the *impotency* of ineffectual change, he found himself too impressionable to refuse a call of need. He offered a few words of blessing to appease their hysterics, confident that simple prayers would ease their doubts. These preconceptions were challenged when he found them quivering, embraced in mutual dependency, refusing to even enter their own home. So *naively* he entered alone…

The rooms were silent and absent. He found himself feeling self-conscious, *ridiculous,* speaking aloud words of blessing without an audience. No sooner had he doubted than the house transformed acutely into a disturbing affair, counteracting his words with *whistles and chills* and the clattering of doors, causing his voice to rise louder and louder to attain mastery over the rowdy din. He pressed from room to room blessing each as he endeavored. In the grand living room ornaments and glass rebelled, reverberating abrasive against the air, the chandelier shattered, fragments whirled at him; he dodged aside and drew his crucifix in defense. In reaction to his affront, a *giant pentangle* appeared on the main wall, pronouncing itself from the surface as though embossed. He experienced a repelling force and aimed his cross in sight of the unholy symbol - they held each other in check. About his feet sharp lines, circles and incantations were drawn at great speed rounding him, and he followed the dissecting marks with his disbelieving eyes until they joined at all points into a continuous web on all four walls, ceiling and the floor; and he in the circle: *the sacrifice.*

He maintained the defense of his holy cross, gripping with both hands to endure the aching duress, arms unwavering in direct conflict with the *Black Force* aggrandized Shape. The surmounting weight brought him to his knees and vied to bow him in *penitence,* he prayed and his crucifix would not submit…

'Christ beside me, Christ before me;
Christ behind me, Christ within me;
Christ beneath me, Christ above me;
Christ to right of me, Christ to left of me;
Christ in my lying, my sitting, my rising;
Christ in heart of all who know me,
Christ on tongue of all who meet me,
Christ in eye of all who see me,
Christ in ear of all who hear me.'

…Faintly at first, vague figure-like shapes *manifested* around the edge of the room, many, three rows deep crowding in a greater circle. Each dressed immaculately in *evening wear,* adorned from a bygone era - but their heads were *Animal* - he knew them to be mask, but they occurred *so* real, so *Alive* - every single one focused on the sacrifice… and then the flickering cloud of shadow that draped about them, from where the candle light could not penetrate, descended the beastly group, seeping from their bodies and hemorrhaging across the floor as though each one was *emptying of blood*. The creeping shadow obliterated the lines and by the time it had reached him, it, and the *ill-made people* faded from sight… Only the pentangle remained, but he felt the greater power *soar* through him and the mark yielded its hand and withdrew back into the wall without trace.

He thought his ordeal over… but as he offered a prayer the words stuck in his throat, he strove only for his *full shouting* words to come out as *whisper,* and he staggered to breathe. Another force vied with him, an entity that had been held as prisoner by the *malevolent supremacy.* Overcome he retreated to the door but the handle was rigid. He shouted all the commands he could muster, but they fell dead on the air, and the exertion, compounded by the tightening round his throat, shuck him. The *whistle* dominated; he couldn't say how long before he realized it was in fact a *scream* - and only when he knew this did he see the *girl* in the sacrificial circle where he had previously stood - and she looked *deep into his eye…*

His inexperienced mistake - to exorcise the house alone, while leaving no door or window open, and with nowhere to go and in desperation, the *girl's spirit* entered him… Part of him knew it, *felt her,* but floundered in denial from the severity and the shame. The Couple bounded in happiness, confident he had cleansed their house of woe, which he had, but he left taking *her* with him. I can't imagine his *tormented,* knowing what had befallen, the doubts, fears, anguish, as if he'd contracted an *insidious disease.* He refused to ask for help and locked himself away, determined to oust the spirit alone; *purging* himself, *flagellating, starving* his body, *racked,* consuming only prayer, hermetically sealed in a *sickness,* willing to *sacrifice* his very heartbeat rather than succumb…

They contested every inch of territory, his mind and body a battlefield of pits and sores, boiling and freezing with the torrent tug of war; *wagering his own annihilation.* The *Girl* was finally given to concede; she revealed herself and bargained for *clemency*. She offered him her gift, a permit to *traverse both worlds,* for hers was where his prey strayed from his reach. Although he was tempted, it was his *empathy* for the Girl, and her plight, that persuaded; for she, like him and I, are cursed to atone before we can ascend. He could not abandon nor turn a blind eye, placing the necessity of another above his own dilemma, and so he gave her a temporary reprieve...

As he began to *know* her, earn respect and understanding - he discovered the *evils* done unto her, how she was *coveted* and *Special,* how she had been *promised to the darkness;* he saw a girl in need of protection, from those who would pervert her *gifts* and corrupt her back to evil, and from those who sought to punish her for resisting their charms and advances. He harbored her in the end out of *humanity* - as if she was a living girl of *flesh and blood* in need of shelter...

In time they no longer communicated as two, but coexisted, able to know and think as one - utilizing their combined strengths and experiences... *and weaknesses...* When his strength would fail, she would carry him through.

I don't believe in *fairy-tales,* that's what I told her, and departed without leave. I couldn't allow myself to believe, couldn't calculate the *implications.* Her story, if only a *grain* of truth, would explain so much, so many of his Herculean deeds.

I asked Clara at City Library to quarry the archives for Milbourne House: the name of old for the location of Fr Cotton's alleged bewitchment. I wanted to know about the Girl, about her family, and how she *died.* Against her loyalties I persuaded Clara to keep her findings from the Priest... She discovered that the Girl's parents were *society* people, their movements recorded in the tittle-tattle and gossip columns of the time; where it was noted that Amelia was in fact their adopted daughter, *Amelia...* Her origin was undetermined, brought back from one of their numerous expeditions - the Americas seemed everyone's best guess. The couple were at the forefront of the spiritualist revival - the rediscovered power that ensnared Conan Doyle and Alistair Crowley, and like the latter they were eventually drawn to the *noxious dominion,* into the cult of Black Magic, Witchcraft and Satanism. They fell from mainstream favour, disappeared and their end remained absent from the records...

Gregory Thorne demanded an audience with a Priest. His request could not be denied. He argued that to receive a *Man of the Cloth* in the visiting room, or his cell, would impinge on his spiritual needs; a compromise of the institute grounds was agreed.

Fr Cotton was escorted around to the rear of the mansion. The manicured lawns were decorated in autumn-fall litter - colours ripe even beyond death, at least for a little while. Gregory sat on a fine pine chair, hands together between his knees, his body *rigid* pressing in on itself as if from a chill - though it was a pleasant late-September day, where even the inconsistent breeze blew *no harm.* His face betrayed his ill-poise, as he smiled favorably and unperturbed. An empty chair awaited on the leafy lawn facing him, gauged to a safe distance. Two strong looking orderlies stood aside the mirroring chairs, within quick reach of their charge.

There was a civilized air to the unwholesome affair. Fr Cotton's escort departed along the dainty pathway back to reception. Dr MacNanmara had pre-warned him and given instruction on the protocol of do's and don'ts. The Priest approached the chair, kicking up rustles of reds and yellow-golds; he sat and faced his opponent; they floated on a Monet painting, a mixing pallet of colours *kissing* the surface of the lawn. Nobody spoke. A Stray leaf was occasionally plucked from a branch by the stuttering breeze and tumbled through the swirl only to settle discarded on the imaginary pond.

'You are here to save me Holy Man...'

Fr Cotton did not respond, he continued to size up the stranger.

Irritated by the Priest's non-responsiveness he quickly forced the issue. 'You will pray for me *Holy Man*. And together we will ask for forgiveness - from a *merciful* Lord... You cannot deny my repentance!'

'*Listen Pal,*' Fr Cotton spoke offering no respect, 'You've no Kudos with me, so don't think you can boss me around.'

Gregory went especially quiet and serpentine, '...I can make life difficult. I have the ear of the masses, the newspapers will gobble you up; your superiors won't want a scandal... your Job is on the line..!'

'My superiors say Screw You! They sent me here to *bury* you... You really want forgiveness... I'm your last chance - *convince me...*'

Gregory's minders shuffled ill at ease, restless on their feet, apprehensive. They shot Fr Cotton a reproachful glance, mindful of his confrontational approach. Gregory Thorne grew tense, implodable; then his muscles melted into the chair and he smiled with resignation.

'Oh Father... We seem to have gotten off on the wrong foot. Forgive my petulance, I am, of course, in your hands... can you guide me unto the righteous path?' He absently kicked crackling leaves away from his chair, as if creating a fissure between the Lilly pads to enable his escape, slipping down the into watery underworld with his own kind.

Fr Cotton measured, by his inner guide, that this one was under no undue influence. The voices in his head, if he had any, were psychological, and not his domain; and if anything, for this reason, he *feared* Thorne even more. Although the garden was calm he felt this man's rigid shoulders suppressing a *hurricane* in his unassuming shell; perhaps that's why he *cramped* so, holding a storm of rage at bay by fragile bonds. If *earthly evil* could be embodied in a man not under the influence of *biblical wickedness* - then it resided in him: he was abominable.

As Cotton sat in silence, quietly judging him, Gregory gauged his conclusion. All emotion was instantly absent from his face…

'You Dirty, Dirty, Dirty, Dirty, Dirty, Little Little Man… I'll come to you. You'll be sorry when I get out, I'll come to you. You'll be Sorry as I piss in your face, as I CUT off your LIPS and your EARS… And your EYELIDS too… You'll be Sorry…'

Fr Cotton stood and walked way, no longer willing to hold eye contact with the unsheathed villainy. Gregory did not follow. The guards came in with haste and locked his arms. He didn't resist until they pulled him to his feet to remove him back to his room.

He *roared* on as they Dragged him away, 'You're gonna SUCK on my SPIT..! I'm gonna stick the *knife* in your God Damed Jesus..! I'm gonna make you all bleed...'

Fr Cotton followed the lonely path back around the grand building reciting to drown out Gregory's talk from his head *'The Lord is my shepherd, I shall not want…'*

Her narrative played on my mind: I pondered her words and motive. I returned for answers, but she's wasn't there: no light, no sign of life; the row a lonely port without her. She was gone without message or *courtesy,* none knowing when, or if she'd return...

And then one evening I recieved an invitation delivered by her chauffeur, a man broad and short, a pin head on a cubist body. Though hesitant, I allowed myself to be escorted, and the *monotone henchman* drove me out of the city, far from civility as the early night fell. We hurtled through claustrophobic hedge lined country lanes, and eerie blacknesses stretching beyond reach, until we reached the cliff-edged abyss, taking hairpin turns outrageously close to the precipice and the cold sea.

She greeted me on the driveway, dismissing her chauffer. To my dismay he reversed and fled, abandoning me to her charity. The corner of her mouth betrayed a wry smile in reply. My eyes embraced her, there, on her private ground, blooming in sympathetic light, her dusky hair untied, draping over her right shoulder in a gentle unraveling twist, floating at ease in her skin and the looseness of her blouse and skirt.

'Come' she spoke pleasantly and I followed her inside. Her second home comfortable and smart, garnished with feminine details; a home she hung her *wanders spirit* at the door. It was here that I noticed that her naked, gloveless forearms were finessed by a softening of *downy hair,* and as my eyes followed her, *kisscurling* wisps delicately waterfell from the back of her neck intriguingly down. The uninitiated may have considered this disclosure an elemental fault, but in truth in never detracted from her for a moment, to the contrary, she carried it audaciously as an affirmation of her very womanhood...

She sipped crimson from a glass, and knew better than to offer me, but I was in no danger of the wanton thirst.

'I've thought a great deal about you since last we talked' she admitted.

'As have I.'

'Do you believe my story now Julian?'

'Some of it checks out' I said without giving my doubts away.

She smiled pleased with herself and touched my arm, 'I'm so glad you've come.'

Setting down her glass, she held her hands out to me. I didn't understand her intent, her gesture too intimate. 'Do I have your permission?' she queried gingerly.

I couldn't reason as to whether she was *making a pass,* or if I was somehow *inappropriate.* She sensed my empty-headedness. Reaching down as I stood dumbly, she took my palms to read, 'Do you mind?' her voice spoke *soothing* and *empathetic.*

I shuck my head having momentarily lost the function of speech. Her penetrating gaze *pierced* deep into my hands; she ran her thumb caressing my *meaningful lines.*

'You are not a kind man, as such, but you have kindness in you… Sensitive is how I would describe it…You'.

Her fingers which had examined so deliberately now fondled for the pleasure of it; her hands ugly but tender as fresh linen.

She led me to the nearby table; brought a hurricane candle over from the mantle. Placing her hand inside the long stem, her digits stretched *distorting* in the flowing glass, until she lit the wick. She laid out my cards chosen from the deck, the pictures ornate, the cards not her own brand but an antique set. We sat silently for a time as she studied all their secrecies… I *suffered* as if *naked,* all my subconscious flaws for her to muse, and the misguided deeds of my *past;* and a future of which she could play *puppeteer* - telling me as little as she wished and withholding the greater knowledge for herself…

She broke concentration, frustrated but resigned to it.

'Julian. You're not interested in my foresight… I had wondered if this was the case. You have no concern for fortune, or *love,* or even the fate of those close to you… All you want is to know whether you are *Saved,* or not! Whether you have *atoned,* earned your place in paradise…'

Her insight caught me off guard, she met my eyes, knowingly, and perhaps even lovingly. 'I know the answer… But I cannot tell you…' If it were at all possible to believe, she appeared both happy and sad.

She hadn't said *wouldn't,* but she *couldn't* tell. As if reading my mind she answered '…It is *forbidden*…'

'Isn't everything you do forbidden,' I replied insensitively.

'Some things are more *illicit* than others: to prophesize about your path in this world is one thing; but to unveil your destiny in the afterlife is the providence of the Gods… One a little white lie, the other a sin of *consequence*… But the answer isn't that simple' she offered compassionately, 'there is an ever present *variable*… You could be Saved today… and condemned tomorrow…

…But no matter which course you undertake, there is a man who will intersect your chart, whether you will it or not; a forthcoming circumstance that will bring you to conflict…' Her mood grew overcast. 'He is known as *The Cardinal;* he will come for Vincent, offering temptations, and you must use all your devices to jeopardize his design.

His spies have been leaches on the Priest ever since his misfortune with the *girl*… He has sought to weaken him; corrupting his allies, tempting them away long before you enrolled. Vincent had been earmarked for a position of repute, had access to powerful men. Then the Cardinal secretly brought him to his knees, until he was friendless and alone, ostracized and downtrodden. For in this lowly position he'd be more pliable, more susceptible to the Cardinal's offer; a sly plan, tactically astute - unless *you* can dissuade him from indirectly handing over his *soul*.

His Eminence,' she spoke bitterly, 'fears him, cannot tolerate a rival: an unsanctioned power on the street. Vincent will have to submit or fold…

If he rebukes the Cardinal's offer, which he must, the Cardinal will no longer distinguish him from the enemy. If you are not on his *side,* you are his foe - there is no charity… He is a powerful adversary, but your adversary he must become.

Don't take my warning lightly Julian, Don't be tempted by

his alliance; it would be less daunting to fight as part of his greater force, rather than Vincent's rag-tag band of rebels and misfits, alone in no-man's land… But I UGRE you to stand on your own, even though there is little help I can give… He is my arch enemy, but I am only a fly to him…'

I permitted myself a series of cascading moments, to breathe, contemplate, and to digest her forewarning.
'Quite a bargain. Seems I have little choice…'
'*Life* is not without peril. Wrong turns lead to consequences beyond our frail skin… There is only *One* choice to take.'
'…This a dark sentence you've handed me.'
'Not I… I'm only the unlucky messenger… And don't resent me for the delivering of bad news,' she pleaded, 'though you have every right. But I sympathize… My every client is a portent of misfortune, ugliness, guilt, and grim secrets. Death and harm… They lay their troubles on me: I see it in there *eyes,* in their *hands,* and in the *cards.* And bad news *lingers…* If I see a mother who will outline her children, I soften the blow, talk in riddles; they think I'm being vague because the future's difficult to read - but it's only kindness. Though some *deserve* to know the truth, and I *TELL* them… But those who suffer I bandage up their hurts and carry them home with me. I see their misfortunes and grievances in my waking dreams… Though this helps,' she said taking another sip from her mysterious cocktail.

'About this time of the evening I like to take a little air… Would you join me to stroll along the beach? We won't be long…'
…She appeared immune to the fret, actively encouraging the breeze to *bellow* her skirt and run its fingers through her hair. I followed behind erasing her *virgin* footprints from the sand. This was indeed a fair creature: a fairy-entity dancing on the shore - leading me beguiled as she blended in and out of the night. She was

an enticing prospect; but even if she were to let me in, she would forever remain unattainable.

She sat down on the cold sand, hugging her knees, looking out pensively into the *deepening sea:* she spoke of an *affinity* with her *cruel neighbour.* I stood at her side, reluctant to but feeling conspicuous I sat down nearby. We were accompanied by the lapping whispers of the tide alone… until she turned and confided.

'There are times, Joon my friend,' she spoke sadly, 'when I paddle out far into the dark waters, under the stars and the moonlight as my witness, not knowing if I'll find the courage to return.' The smile that had departed returned again bashful, casting aside her woe… I risked a kiss - there's no *crueler rebuff* than lips declined, but I stuck my neck out on a limb. She only left me hanging in the breeze for a moment, and then encountered my mouth, though only dutifully.

'You can call me *Bethany…*' she whispered longingly from the shadow of her face I couldn't penetrate.

She stood defiantly, shaking off more than the sand, 'Come!' Taking my hand we walked meandering without conversation back to her secret home.

Our silent collusion preserved; I mimed the collaborating prisoner; she circled blowing out the candles, and then led me to the bedroom. One last kindled flame she cradled in a long glass lampstem, smoldering in a *low burn* - enough to find our way, enough to keep us *strangers.*

We joined to smother the latent chill that had accompanied us home, lingering around unprotected neck, toe and ankle. We radiated, agitating our lips and bodies, grappling cohesively in our heedless pod. Her body was all woman; in the half-light I guessed at tracery tattoos hidden away, leading to her *delicate places* - from which her downy softness grew whispering curls to lap her navel. She was *exotic,* a delight, she was giving, and for a brief moment she was mine.

I coveted her lifestyle: the beach house and the sea at her call; a humble janitor, I could have spent an eternity there just watching her walk with the sand between her toes.

I'd forgotten the weight of woes upon me, lost in the corners of her lips.

Slipping out from under the sheet she vanished from the bedroom, and then returned carrying a long stemmed shot glass which held a *sap green* liqueur, *luminous* in the iridescent candle strain. She slid in next to my radiating heat; I felt the cold pimples arisen on her surface skin. She offered me the cocktail, I declined, unsure of its contents.

'Drink it, make you Good inside.'

She *slinked* her naked body atop of mine, then emptied the contents into her mouth in one slug. She kissed, releasing the *potent* cocktail into me, mixing with her tongue before I *swallowed*... I wanted another, wanted her mouth to *trick me* again, but I found I couldn't lift my heavy sleep begging head...

I awoke in my own bed, dressed and on the covers. I lay half dazed, *fading in and out;* seemed to take an exaggerated time to bring the world into focus... And then it hit me - the precious memory of there and her... Thought I could still *taste* her, but only the residue of her pretty *poison,* and the numb feeling of her body nuzzling into mine - the ghost of instant *nostalgia...*

I found her note, it read:

Don't look for me again.
It's not forthcoming.

Fate is a delicate mistress x

Did she *play* me..? Undoubtedly… A man would be wise to distrust every word from her *witching lips*… But I wanted to believe, and if that was my downfall, then I chose it…

But yet rejoice not in this, that spirits are subject unto you: but rejoice in this, that your names are written in heaven.
Luke 10: 20
Douay-Rheims Bible

Printed in the United Kingdom by
Lightning Source UK Ltd., Milton Keynes
138005UK00002B/187/P